Batting Order

A
HOME TEAM
NOVEL

Batting Order

MIKE LUPICA

SIMON & SCHUSTER BOOKS FOR YOUNG READERS
NEW YORK LONDON TORONTO SYDNEY NEW DELHI

SIMON & SCHUSTER BOOKS FOR YOUNG READERS
An imprint of Simon & Schuster Children's Publishing Division
1230 Avenue of the Americas, New York, New York 10020
SIMON & SCHUSTER BOOKS FOR YOUNG READERS
is a trademark of Simon & Schuster, Inc.
For information about special discounts for bulk purchases, please contact Simon & Schuster
Special Sales at 1-866-506-1949 or business@simonandschuster.com.
The Simon & Schuster Speakers Bureau can bring authors to your live event.
For more information or to book an event, contact the Simon & Schuster Speakers Bureau
at 1-866-248-3049 or visit our website at www.simonspeakers.com.
Book design by Greg Stadnyk
The text for this book was set in Adobe Garamond Pro.
Manufactured in the United States of America
0419 FFG
First Edition
2 4 6 8 10 9 7 5 3 1
Library of Congress Cataloging-in-Publication Data
Names: Lupica, Mike, author.
Title: Batting order / Mike Lupica.
Description: First edition. | New York : Simon & Schuster Books for Young Readers, [2019] |
Summary: Twelve-year-old Matt Baker is the best all-rounder on his baseball team, but
can he help Big Ben Roberson improve his hitting and stand up to his father?
Identifiers: LCCN 2018033652 (print) | LCCN 2018040055 (eBook)
| ISBN 9781534421554 (hardcover) | ISBN 9781534421578 (eBook)
Subjects: | CYAC: Baseball—Fiction. | Stuttering—Fiction. | Self-confidence—Fiction. |
Parent and child—Fiction. | Single-parent families—Fiction.
Classification: LCC PZ7.L97914 (eBook) | LCC PZ7.L97914 Bc 2019 (print) |
DDC [Fic]—dc23
LC record available at https://lccn.loc.gov/2018033652

This book is for my children: Hannah, Christopher, Alex, and Zach. If there really were a Way Back Machine, I wish I could get in it and coach them all in their favorite sports, just one more time.

Batting Order

ONE

He'd always felt big on a baseball field.

It was the thing Matt Baker loved the most about the game. There were no height requirements or size requirements. Matt remembered one time, when he was younger, his mom had taken him to Universal Studios in Florida. There was a *Back to the Future* ride, named after one of her favorite old movies. But you had to be a certain height to go on the ride. Matt wasn't. He'd never even heard of the movie. But he never forgot the woman at the door telling him that he was too small.

Baseball wasn't like that. It didn't care how tall you were. Or how short.

In the big leagues, you could be as tall as home run hitters like Aaron Judge or Giancarlo Stanton, who one season had combined to hit 110 home runs. But you could also be five-foot-six the way José Altuve, Matt's favorite player in the world, was. And Matt knew there were a lot of baseball fans who were not convinced that Altuve, the Astros second baseman, was really even five-six.

It didn't matter. The year Aaron Judge hit fifty-one home runs for the Yankees and won the Home Run Derby at the All-Star Game, he only finished second in the Most Valuable Player voting. José Altuve finished first. Judge was more than a foot taller than Altuve. And Giancarlo Stanton, who won the MVP in the National League that year because he hit fifty-nine home runs, was six-six. It made him a foot taller than José Altuve, exactly.

Baseball didn't care. It was why the season, first in the spring with his regular Little League team in South Shore and then in the summer with All-Stars, was Matt Baker's favorite time of the year. It was his birthday, and Christmas.

Baseball didn't only make him feel like his biggest self. It made him feel like his very best self. For Matt, it wasn't just about being the second baseman and the all-around player he wanted to be. Baseball made him feel like the confident *person* he wanted to be. It didn't matter that he was the shortest guy on all the teams he'd played on so far, and the shortest guy in sixth grade this past year at South Shore Middle School.

But there was something else.

Matt had stuttered for most of his life. He knew that he stuttered less on a ball field than anywhere else. Somehow the words didn't stop as often. Sometimes Matt thought it was because he was too busy trying to show everybody—and himself—that he wasn't going to let his lack of size stop him.

This spring he had hit .500 exactly for his Little League team, the Nationals, as they'd won their league championship. He'd led off for the Nationals and played second. His teammates all told him after the season that if the league gave out an MVP award, he would have won it the same way his guy Altuve had won it with the Astros, while they were in the process of winning their first World Series in the history of that franchise.

Matt knew he hadn't been the player everybody remembered best from that Nationals team, despite all the hits he had gotten and all the times he'd been on base because of walks. He knew they remembered some of the long home runs the team's first baseman, Big Ben Roberson, had hit. Even though that meant they also forgot how many times Ben had struck out taking his big cuts.

Ben struck out three times in the Nationals' championship game against the Rockies. But that isn't what everyone talked about when the game was over and the championship trophy had been presented. No, everyone remembered a fifth-inning home run when the game was still tied. It was a home run that so many adults at the game, so many of whom had grown up in South Shore themselves, said was the longest they'd ever seen someone Ben's age hit at Healey Park.

So there was a *lot* of talk about that after the game, and not so much about Matt getting two singles and a double and a walk and scoring every time he'd been on base. But that was fine with Matt. Ben did most of the talking. He liked to talk, often about himself. That was fine with Matt too. They were teammates, but they'd never become close friends.

As different as his style was from Ben's, Matt did enjoy watching Ben hit. He liked the way everything seemed to stop on the field when Ben stepped to the plate, because people knew something dramatic was likely about to happen, for one team or the other, strikeout or long ball. It was, Matt knew, one of the things he loved about all sports, really: The next moment was the one that could change everything. Ben made you feel that way every time he stepped to the plate. Even if he did strike out, he'd still come back to the bench smiling.

"All it takes is one," he'd say after he struck out.

Matt didn't think Ben loved baseball the way he did football and basketball, especially basketball, where he was already a star in his travel league. Sometimes Matt thought Ben just played baseball because it was something fun to do in the spring and summer. But you still wanted him on your team, and not just because of the home runs. If you were an infielder the way Matt was, you loved having him at first base. With his size and reach, he made you think it was practically impossible to make a throw that Ben couldn't catch. Their coach, John Sargent—everybody just called him Sarge—liked to say that the only things Ben couldn't catch at first base were low-flying birds.

The truth was that Ben was a lot more consistent catching balls than hitting them.

But there was a different kind of bond between Sarge and Matt. It was Sarge who called Matt "The Little Engine That Could." Sarge who kept telling Matt that if you added up all of Matt's hits and walks and even the times when his speed would cause an infielder on the other team to rush a throw and make an error, his on-base percentage was nearly a thousand.

Matt would tell his coach that he didn't care how he got on base, as long as he got on base.

"I know you're happy to take a walk," Sarge had been saying to Matt the night before at practice. "But my favorite thing is when they finally make a pitch to you that's too good, and you show them how much pop you have in your bat. How much stronger you are than you look."

In that moment, all Matt wanted to say was, "Thank you."

But he could not.

The first word just wouldn't come right away. The feeling, he knew by now, would come on him without notice. He would be stuck again. A lot of times it was a simple word that began with *t*.

Or *th*.

Sometimes it was just a simple "thanks."

Sometimes the best he could do was smile, because the word just couldn't get out of him.

He did that with Sarge last night. Sarge smiled back at him.

"Not going anywhere," he said.

Finally, and slowly, Matt said, "Thank you."

Then they were back to talking baseball, and the words were spilling out of Matt, and he told Sarge, "I feel like my power is my secret weapon."

Sarge was still smiling. "It won't be for long once we start playing games. They'll all find out that big things really do come in small packages."

Matt had heard that one before. Had been hearing it his whole life. He was used to it by now. The funny thing was that his dad, who'd divorced his mom when Matt was five and was living in London now, was six feet two inches tall. He'd been a home run hitter when he was Matt's age, and all the way through high school. But he hadn't been a big part of Matt's life long enough to see Matt become the ballplayer he had. Even when Matt remembered his mom telling him she loved him exactly the way he was—meaning the size he was—his dad hardly ever said anything. *There were so many things,* Matt thought now, *that he didn't know about me.*

Kevin Baker had remarried after moving to London, and now had a son with his new wife. He'd e-mail Matt once in a while. He'd usually remember to send a gift on his birthday and Christmas, though he'd missed a few birthdays.

He didn't know how good Matt had become in baseball. If he even knew Matt stuttered, Matt's mom, Rachel, had never mentioned it. Sometimes you heard people talk about "single" parents. Matt thought of his mom as his only parent.

She loved baseball, too. Even though she was barely five

feet tall, she'd been a star softball pitcher at South Shore High School and then at the University of North Carolina, where she'd even gotten a softball scholarship.

People made a big thing about "soccer moms." Matt's was a baseball mom, through and through.

From the time that Matt Baker—he hated it when people called him Matty—had first started playing T-ball, she had told him the same thing.

"They say that size matters in sports," she said. "Well, guess what, it does: the size of your talent and the size of your heart."

Matt had read up a lot on the history of baseball. He knew that Joe Morgan, one of the greatest second basemen of all time, was only an inch taller than Altuve. And Joe Morgan had played with one of the best teams of all time, a Cincinnati Reds squad known as "The Big Red Machine." He was a little guy who had ended up in the Hall of Fame.

Size didn't hold Joe Morgan back. It wasn't holding José Altuve back. Matt, with his own strong baseball heart, was determined that it wasn't going to hold him back.

Still:

There was a part of him that thought it must be nice to be as big as Ben Roberson, even though in his heart he knew he was a better baseball player.

Ben had a personality that seemed to match his size,

MIKE LUPICA

whether he was with kids his own age, or adults. Matt looked at him and saw somebody whose whole life seemed to be a home run, even when he had swung and missed again.

And no matter what, Big Ben Roberson never seemed to be at a loss for words.

TWO

Matt didn't stutter all the time.

He began to notice it when he was in first grade, and then it was a part of him.

It was always worse if he had to stand up and say something in front of his class, or if he was called on by one of his teachers to answer a question when he wasn't expecting it. By now he knew all the words to describe what would happen to him. He'd get "blocked." Or "stuck." He knew exactly what it felt like when a word would be frozen in his throat, or on his lips, and simply would not come out right away. It didn't matter how fast his brain was working. It didn't matter that he knew what he wanted to say, or that he knew the answer.

Then he would be in the same old situation: trying to slow down, even when he wanted the moment to pass quickly. On a ball field, his speed set him apart from other players, no matter what their size. He was able to run the bases faster. He was able to get the ball out of his glove faster to make a throw. He knew everybody talked about his bat speed.

But when the words wouldn't come he had to do the opposite. His speech-language pathologist, Ms. Francis, was constantly telling him to *slow do*wn. Eventually the word, or words, would come out. It was like being in a car with his mom when a light turned green. He would feel like he was in motion again.

Always, Matt would feel a tremendous sense of relief.

Almost as if he could breathe again.

Stuttering was another reason why the Houston Astros had become his favorite team in the world. Because if José Altuve was his favorite player, the Astros center fielder, George Springer, was his second. During the World Series, Springer hit five home runs and became the Series MVP.

George Springer stuttered.

Matt had read up on George Springer a lot. In just about

every story about him, he always said pretty much the same thing:

"Don't call it a speech impediment, because I've never looked at it as an impediment."

"It doesn't hold me back," George Springer had said in one of the articles Matt read. "Some people have blue eyes, some people have blond hair, some don't. Some people stutter and some don't."

Matt remembered all of that, word for word. He'd even written it down on an index card that he kept in the top drawer of the desk in his bedroom. George Springer refused to see stuttering as an impediment, just like José Altuve didn't let his size be an impediment to becoming one of the best players in the major leagues.

One of them became the league MVP.

One of them became the World Series MVP.

It was all Matt Baker needed to know, and to hope, and to dream, even though it was hard sometimes. Matt was a fighter. He knew his teammates always had his back, and not just because he was such a good player. His classmates, especially the ones he had grown up with, never made fun of him because he stuttered, or laughed at him. His mom always taught him to believe in himself. So did Sarge, who had coached him this spring and was about to coach him in All-Stars.

So did Ms. Sue Francis, his speech pathologist.

Matt knew he had good coaches. He knew he had good friends. He knew he had a great mom. He knew how much he had going for him in his life. He did.

But even though he never said this to his coaches, or his friends, or his teammates, or his mom, he knew himself well enough to know that no matter how much he fought his stuttering, it was just another thing that could make him feel small.

There were other things that did it too. His father not being in his life was a big one.

But stuttering was bigger.

THREE

They were practicing again tonight at Healey Park, the second practice for their All-Star team, which would be called the Astros.

When Matt had found out, he couldn't believe it. You didn't get to select your team name in their league. It was completely random: one of the members of the league's board of directors picked the names out of a hat. Because of where South Shore was located, there were a lot of Yankees fans on the team, and Red Sox fans, and Mets fans. He was the only Astros fan. But now his team was going to be called the South Shore Astros. This was a good sign. Maybe even a great one.

Not only would they be the Astros, but he was going to get to wear number 27, José Altuve's number. Sarge had taken care of that for him.

"Now that doesn't mean that you have to spend the whole season first-pitch swinging the way your guy Altuve does," Sarge told him.

"But I can do it sometimes, right?" Matt said.

"Knowing you, you'll know when," Sarge said.

Three of Matt's teammates from the spring would be with him on the Astros. Kyle Sargent, the coach's son, would be at third base. Their center fielder would be Denzel Lincoln. Big Ben would be at first and batting cleanup.

One of Matt's favorite players from the spring, José Dominguez, would be their shortstop. José had played for the Yankees, the team the Nationals had beaten in the championship game, and been both their best hitter and fielder. He had even hit a three-run homer in the bottom of the last inning to cut a 5–1 Nationals lead to 5–4 and make Matt and his teammates sweat out two more outs. The Yankees had put two runners on with two outs, but Matt ended the game with a diving stop to his left, throwing out the baserunner from his knees.

But now José was his teammate, and a perfect match for him on the other side of second base. Matt batted leadoff for the Nationals, but now Sarge had decided to bat him third in front of Big Ben, José ahead of him, and lead off with Denzel, who was the fastest player they had, on the bases and in the outfield.

"I'm not going to make a big announcement about this," Sarge said. "But the way I look at baseball, you bat your best hitter third."

When Matt told José about the batting order, José high-fived him right away.

"With you and the big guy coming after me, all I'm going to see all season are fat pitches," he said. "I am one happy dude."

They were standing near second base, waiting to go through their infield drills.

"How about me?" Matt said. "I don't just have you getting on base ahead of me, I've got you right next to me in the field."

"I've got your back, you've got mine," José said.

They waited for Sarge to start hitting them ground balls, but he was still talking to Stone Russell. It gave Matt a chance to explain to José, whom he hadn't really talked to very much when they were playing against each other, that he stuttered, and that there would be times when he had trouble getting words out, even during games.

José smiled.

"Same thing happens to me sometimes, for a different reason," he said.

"What reason?" Matt said.

"My family came here from Puerto Rico," he said. "My parents still mostly like to speak Spanish at home. So sometimes I can't find the words either."

Matt said, "We should get along fine."

José was still smiling.

"I'm not much of a talker on the field anyway," José said.

Then Sarge told them to take their positions. The next sound they heard was the crack of his bat as he hit a ground ball to his son at third base. The only chatter came from Sarge. The summer night sounded just perfect to Matt.

As usual, everything changed when it was time for Ben to take batting practice.

The infielders and outfielders took a few steps back when Ben stepped into the batter's box. The infielders, Matt included, suddenly looked *extremely* alert, on the chance that Ben might hit a ball right at them instead of elevating one over the fence. Matt knew Ben wasn't much of a line drive hitter. But when he did hit one, he could hit a baseball hard enough to knock the glove off a guy's hands. It had nearly happened to Matt at their first practice. Ben, a right-handed hitter who hardly ever went the opposite way, hit one right at Matt. He was ready for it. The ball didn't knock the glove off his hand. But when Matt took a quick look at his palm after throwing the ball back in to Stone Russell, it was the color of strawberry ice cream.

There was one other thing that always happened when it was Ben's turn to hit:

It was as if somebody had turned up the volume on the chatter coming from both the outfield and the infield, including from Matt. For some reason, and for all the work he did with Ms. Francis on slowing himself down when the words wouldn't come, somehow his fast chatter from second base was never a problem. Maybe it was because he didn't feel as if his was the only voice on the field. He was just part of the group.

"*What you got tonight, big man?*"

"*Tell the guys on the back field to look out.*"

"*Batter, batter, batter.*"

"*Don't swing and miss, big man, the breeze might knock us all over.*"

"*Give him your heater, Sarge.*"

MIKE LUPICA

"Wait, does Sarge even still have *a heater?"*

"Shouldn't that swing count for two strikes instead of one?"

To Matt, it was like baseball rap. He liked real rap. But he loved it on a ball field like this.

Ben, even though he had swung right through Sarge's first few pitches, was smiling. After he swung and missed again, and the chatter level increased a little more, he stepped out of the box, still smiling, and made a motion to his teammates in the field that said, "Bring it on."

He looked down at Kyle at third base and said, "You better hope I don't pull one, dog."

Kyle laughed—a little nervously, Matt thought.

"If you're trying to scare me," Kyle said, "you just did!"

Matt knew what he was feeling, having been Ben's teammate with the Nationals. There was nothing scarier than being a runner on third when Ben was just sixty feet away with a bat in his hands. Even though you knew he could pull a line drive and score you, Matt would find himself hoping for either a home run or a fly ball. He told his mom about his feelings one time and she laughed.

"Safety first," she said.

Matt never said anything to Ben, but he knew that if Ben could ever figure out a way to cut down on his swing, he would be a much more dangerous hitter, and a much tougher out. It was what Aaron Judge had done the year he busted out with his fifty-one homers for the Yankees. He had better bat control, he had a better sense of the strike zone, and he still hit his homers. He just struck out a lot less than he had before that.

Ben's swing was still as big as he was.

He connected with the fifth pitch he saw from Sarge. And as soon as Matt heard the sound of the ball on the fat part of Ben's aluminum bat, he didn't even have to turn. Oh, but he did turn, because Matt wanted to watch the flight of the ball.

There was another practice going on at Healey's back field. Matt smiled as he watched Ben's ball land between the center fielder and the right fielder, and go rolling toward their second baseman.

"Did you see where that sucker landed?" Kyle yelled.

"Wait," José said. "The ball *landed*?"

Sarge had turned to watch the flight of the ball himself, and when he turned back to Ben he said, "That one feel okay?"

"Can't lie, coach," he said. "It didn't stink."

Still smiling.

Forget what it's like being that size and that strong, Matt thought to himself. *What is it like being able to hit a baseball that far?*

Ben hit one more home run, though not nearly as far as the first one. He didn't put another one in play. He didn't even

MIKE LUPICA

hit a foul ball. He finished with four more swings and misses. He thought he was done, but then Sarge said, "Let me throw you a few extra pitches, and instead of trying to hit one all the way to Glenbrook, let's pretend we've got the winning run on base, and all you need is a single."

"Shorten my swing, you mean?" Ben said.

"Just a little," Sarge said.

"I can't," Ben said.

"Sure you can, Ben," Sarge said. "You just haven't learned how."

"I'll try," Ben said. "But my dad taught me to hit a certain way. You know what they talk about on TV all the time. He wants me to elevate."

"All I can ask is that you try," Sarge said, ignoring the part about Ben's dad. "It's something we can work on a little bit at a time, big man."

Ben stepped out. Matt watched him from second base, saw how hard he was concentrating as he took some shorter, more level practice swings, exaggerating hitting down on the ball instead of using his normal uppercut.

Sarge threw him more than a few extra pitches. But the harder Ben tried to just put the ball in play, the worse it seemed to get for him. The best he could do, on the last pitch, was a weak ground ball to Kyle.

Ben ran the ball out, all the way through first base even though Kyle had thrown him out easily. But as Ben crossed the base, Matt could see the frustration on his face. The kid who could smile his way through almost anything looked angry at himself.

About ten minutes later, it was Matt's turn to hit, Sarge making him the last batter tonight. Of the ten pitches Matt saw from Sarge, he hit a couple of line drives up the middle, two to right, two to left. He fouled two pitches off, hit another ball right over second base. Then on the last pitch he saw he really connected, on the fat part of his own Easton bat, right on the sweet spot. The ball didn't go over the fence in left-center. It did hit high up off the fence out there.

Not all I got, Matt thought to himself.

But close enough.

Since it was Matt's last swing, he was running all the way, thinking double as he rounded first. But he was watching Denzel the whole time, and when the ball bounced away from him a little, Matt didn't even slow down as he cut the bag at second base, knowing this was going to be a stand-up triple, even in practice.

But when he got to third, he slid into the bag just for the sheer fun of it. It was like he was ending BP tonight with his own exclamation point.

MIKE LUPICA

After he cleaned the dirt off himself, he jogged toward the bench on the first-base side of the field. When he got there, Ben came over to him and said in a quiet voice, "Maybe it wouldn't kill me to hit a little bit more like you."

Ben grinned then.

"Just don't tell the other guys," he said.

FOUR

For his birthday his mom had gotten Matt a subscription to MLB Network, which was pure heaven. It meant that on any given night he could watch any game he wanted on his laptop until it was time to go to bed.

And sometimes, even after that.

Matt liked watching games on TV, sometimes with his mom after dinner. But he was just as happy later in his bed, picking out a game from Houston or Chicago or Cincinnati or Boston or Cleveland or Baltimore. He could go to Minute Maid Park in Houston for an Astros game, or Wrigley Field in Chicago, or Progressive Field in Cleveland. Sometimes, with his door shut, Matt would not only watch the games, but pretend he was doing the color commentary on them. His favorite thing was when he'd be a step ahead of the announcers, calling for a hit-and-run or steal or squeeze play.

He loved it when that would happen.

Alone in his room, alone with baseball, he never had any trouble getting the words out. He never got stopped the way he did in class, when he'd feel a familiar panic come over him. He knew it would pass. He knew the words would eventually come.

He just didn't know when.

But when he was alone in his room with baseball, he was always sure of himself. If it was a day when his team hadn't practiced and he hadn't gotten a chance to even play catch with one of his friends, watching these games at night was the happiest part of his day.

Tonight he watched the Astros play Cleveland. It meant that not only were José Altuve and Carlos Correa in the game, but so was Francisco Lindor, the Indians shortstop, another one of the best young players in the big leagues.

Sarge liked to say how lucky it was to be a baseball fan right now, because he honestly felt there was more young talent in the game than at any other time in its history.

"Hey, you're only twelve," Sarge had said to Matt the day he told him he was going to bat him third. "Some of these guys will still only be in their thirties if you make it to the big leagues."

"Right, coach," Matt said. "You mean when I grow up?"

"That's exactly what I mean," Sarge said.

The game Matt was watching was in the top of the fourth, Astros and Indians tied 2–2, when he got the text from Ben Roberson, who Matt couldn't remember *ever* texting him before.

U doing anything tomorrow?

Matt hit him right back.

Nah.

As soon as he did, he could see on the screen that Ben was answering.

Meet on the field at Healey, like 11?

Matt decided to call him.

MIKE LUPICA

"What's up?" he said.

"I thought we could maybe do some work together," Ben said.

"If you're talking about baseball, I never think of it as work," Matt said. "My mom says that nobody ever says they're going to work baseball. They say they're going to play."

"Maybe we can do a little bit of both tomorrow," Ben said. "Maybe Sarge is right, and I could do some work shortening my swing."

Yes! Matt thought. But he didn't say that.

"I'm down," is what he said.

"Great," Ben said. "See you tomorrow."

Matt was glad to help him, if he could. If somehow Ben became a better hitter, their Astros would be a better team. He'd heard A.J. Hinch, the Astros manager, say once on television that the most important part of his job was putting his players in the best possible position to win.

Matt wasn't a manager. He wasn't a coach. But maybe there was a way to help Ben. Maybe not all dreams had to be big ones.

Maybe you had to start small.

FIVE

The day was so perfect, not too hot, no clouds in the sky. So often you heard the announcers talking about baseball weather.

Well, Matt thought, *today really is baseball weather.*

He was wearing his favorite T-shirt, one his mom had bought for him, a black Astros shirt with an orange star on the front. Since he knew he wouldn't be doing any sliding, he was wearing a pair of gym shorts and rubber cleats. He had his bat with him, and batting gloves, and a couple of water bottles in his bat bag, and even a peanut butter sandwich he'd made for himself. If Ben was ready to work into the afternoon, so was he. As usual when it came to baseball, Matt was ready to go all day.

They had agreed to meet on the back field. The Bakers lived only a couple of blocks from Healey Park, so Matt had ridden his bike over. Ben was waiting on the back field when he got there. Ben was wearing shorts too, and a pretty cool T-shirt of his own, one with the Big Ben clock from London on the front.

He was also wearing a navy blue Yankees cap, with the white NY on the front. Ben said he'd almost had no choice when he was growing up. His dad had been born in the Bronx, New York, practically in the shadow, Ben said, of the old Yankee Stadium. So he was a Yankees fan and Ben's two brothers were Yankees fans. The Yankees, Ben had told Matt one time, were practically a family business for the Robersons.

"What are we going to do if the Astros and Yankees keep going up against each other in the playoffs?" Matt said, pointing up at Ben's cap.

"Root like heck for our teams," Ben said, grinning, "and trash talk the heck out of each other."

"Sounds good," Matt said.

"Of course, I'm better at trash talk than you are," Ben said.

"Tell me about it," Matt said.

He started to get stuck on the *t* in "tell." No reason. But by now he knew he didn't need a reason. It just happened. And sometimes kept happening. He managed to slow himself down just enough, like he was unlocking a door, and got the words out. He didn't want anything to get in his way today. He mostly wanted to get out of his own way.

"Judge has made me even more of a Yankees fan than I was already," Ben said.

"He cut down on his swing," Matt said.

"But he didn't do it until he got to the big leagues," Ben said.

Ben shook his head, as if he were already frustrated about his own swing before they even started today.

"Sometimes I almost feel as if I'm closing my eyes and hoping I get lucky enough to make contact," he said.

"Maybe we can figure out a way to get you to make the kind of contact you did last night *without* getting lucky," Matt said.

"At least one of us has a good attitude about this," Ben said.

"You're here," Matt said.

"Yeah," Ben said. "I guess I am."

Matt saw five or six old balls in the grass next to Ben. He'd told him to bring as many as he could. Matt had brought about the same number himself. He figured they had enough so they wouldn't have to keep stopping to chase them when it was time for Ben to do some hitting.

MIKE LUPICA

"You sure I'm not wasting my time and yours today?" Ben said.

Matt wanted to tell him no, he wasn't.

But now he was blocked for real, and couldn't tell him anything.

"N-n-."

He felt as if his tongue were glued to the roof of his mouth.

But suddenly Ben was acting impatient that Matt couldn't get the word "no" out of his mouth.

"I know, I know," Ben said, "you want to tell me that I'm not wasting my time."

"Yes" was the word that came out then for Matt.

Then he took a deep breath and said, "Make a deal with you. I'll try to help you with your swing. But you have to promise not to help me when I stutter. Because that doesn't help me."

He saw a look come across Ben's face that he didn't understand. For a second he thought maybe the guy who wanted to correct things wrong with his swing didn't want to be corrected anywhere else.

"I just saw you were struggling," Ben said.

"I have to get through it on my own," Matt said.

"Yeah," Ben said, "but I was just trying to help."

"Thank you," Matt said. "But I've got to work it out myself. It means that sometimes you have to wait for me."

"Okay," Ben said, as if wanting to change the subject. "But do you think *you* can help *me*?"

"Yes," Matt said.

The word came out quickly. But for once Matt Baker wondered if saying something, about baseball this time, was going to be a lot easier than doing it.

SIX

Matt had gone on the Internet the night before and done some reading. It was almost like he was doing homework, though he would be the one trying to teach a class to Ben. It wasn't a hardship. Matt loved reading about baseball, not just facts and figures, but history, too. He loved looking up players he heard the announcers talking about, even ones who'd played long before Matt was born.

And Matt loved going on YouTube and finding videos with

coaching tips. His mom knew a lot about proper technique, for both hitting and fielding and even throwing. So did Sarge, who had not just been a great shortstop at South Shore High School, but had gone on to play college baseball, too.

They had taught him a lot. But Matt had taught himself, too, just by doing his own studying. He had learned little tips about fielding, and how to position your feet so you got the best possible running start when you took off from a base. It was all the little stuff, he knew, that could turn out to be huge in a big moment in a game.

"Soooo," Matt said, "I've maybe got some ideas about how you can shorten your swing."

"My dad keeps telling me that if I decide to stick with baseball, I can figure stuff like that out later," Ben said, "but for now to keep swinging for the benches."

Matt couldn't believe what he'd just heard: *If I decide to stick with baseball?* He knew how good Ben was at other sports. Everybody in town who'd seen Ben play knew. But how could somebody who had it in him to give baseballs a ride the way he could ever think about walking away from the game without finding out just how good he could be?

"He's a big golfer, my dad," Ben continued. "He says that the pro who taught him how to play when he was our age, told him to swing as hard as he could. He said the pro told him that you could always make a swing shorter, but that you could never make it bigger. So he's applying that to baseball now. And to me."

"I don't know anything about golf," Matt said.

"I always tell my dad that the ball doesn't move in golf, but he doesn't care," Ben said. "His favorite expression comes from some old golfer who used to say, 'Grip it and rip it.' That's what my dad wants me to do in baseball."

"You can change if you want to," Matt said.

He wasn't sure that was true. But Matt knew that if he didn't try to be positive, Ben was never going to buy in either.

"It's gonna take some work," Matt said.

"But sports are supposed to be fun," Ben said.

"The better you get, the more fun they are," Matt said.

The first thing he did was take Ben's own Easton bat away from him and hand him Matt's much lighter version.

"You're not even letting me use my own *bat*?" Ben said.

"Not today," he said, grinning at Ben.

Matt knew his bat would be way too whippy for Ben in a real game, the way he knew he'd never be able to get Ben's bat around if he was facing real pitching. But from the studying up he'd done on YouTube last night, Matt learned that the key for Ben was simple:

Maintain the bat speed he already had, just using a much more compact swing.

He and Ben collected all the balls and went over to home plate. Matt asked Ben to hand him his bat back, then got into the right-hand batter's box. He told Ben to kneel to the right of the plate, just a little bit up the first base line, and toss balls underhand to him.

"I'm going to get better with somebody pitching *underhand* to me?" Ben said.

"I just want to show you what we're going to work on," Matt said.

Matt didn't set his hands the way he normally did when he was hitting. Instead he placed the end of his bat as close to his right ear as he could get it, with the handle pointing almost straight down at the ground.

"You look like you're trying to stick that bat *in* your ear," Ben said. "No way you can hit a ball like that."

"Way," Matt said.

No hesitation. If he didn't trust this, Ben wouldn't either.

He asked Ben to toss him a pitch, waist high if Ben could manage it, right over the plate. It took Ben a couple of times to put the ball where he wanted and where Matt wanted, but he finally got it right. Matt knew there was only one rule with this drill: You couldn't take the bat back. You had to just come forward with it and, hopefully, drive the ball.

Matt did that now, and connected, the ball making that

sweet sound on his bat, going over the pitcher's mound into short center field.

"No way!" Ben said again.

"Way," Matt said again.

They did it a few more times. Matt didn't hit every ball well. He missed some. This stance and this approach felt as awkward to him as he knew they would to Ben. After a few minutes, he stopped to try to explain the purpose of the drill. He told himself this was just baseball. Even though he had turned this part of Healey Park into a classroom, Matt reminded himself he wasn't making a presentation in front of the class. Just keep it simple, Matt told himself.

For both of us.

"By not taking the bat back," Matt said, "you force your hands to go faster through the hitting zone."

He looked up at Ben.

"Does that make sense to you?" he said.

"I *guess* so," Ben said.

But he didn't sound convinced.

"This teaches you to use your hands and arms in the right way and not waste a lot of motion," Matt said, "and still being able to explode on the ball like you do."

"Show me again," Ben said.

Matt did.

And then again.

And again. It was like Sarge would say when the words wouldn't come for Matt Baker.

He had all day.

Matt hit a few more line drives, some of them surprisingly hard. Then he told Ben to start flipping him the balls faster between swings, so he had less time to think about what he was doing, and was forced to just react to the ball. "See ball, hit ball," Matt's mom liked to say when she'd help Matt work on his hitting.

"You make it look easy," Ben said.

"It's not," Matt said. "But now it's your turn."

"I'm telling you," Ben said, "I'll never be able to do this."

"You won't know until you try."

Matt took his place to the right of the plate, balls in the grass next to him.

It didn't go well.

Matt tossed the balls as softly as he could, imagining himself putting them on a tee. But no matter how softly he tossed the ball, Ben missed.

Then again.

And again.

"Relax," Matt said finally, trying not to sound like a baseball dad.

"I *hate* when people tell me to relax," Ben said, his voice as tight as his grip. Matt could see the guy who went around smiling all the time was gritting his teeth now.

"One of the things the coach said on this video I watched," Matt said, "was that another key to this drill is keeping your hands and arms as relaxed as possible."

"Easy for you to say," Ben said.

"I'm just saying w-w . . ."

Suddenly they were both stressed. Ben started to say something. Matt could see him stop himself.

But Matt was the one who stopped, even putting a hand up. He managed to take in some air, then more.

"I was just saying what the coach on the video said," Matt said to Ben.

"Easy for *him* to say," Ben said.

"Just not me," Matt said.

Ben eventually started to make contact, if feeble contact at first. He wasn't hitting the balls very far. But at least he was hitting some. Finally he hit one line drive that would have gone over the shortstop's head and into left field in a game.

But then he went back to missing.

"I can't do this," he said. "This is *never* going to feel natural. I'm just gonna go back to gripping and ripping."

"You can't give up yet," Matt said. "What you're doing is

exaggerated. You won't swing like this in BP, or even in a game. But if we keep working on it, your swing will just naturally get shorter."

"No, it won't," Ben said.

"I don't want to fight with you," Matt said.

"The only fight going on," Ben said, "is between me and me."

"But if you get better, it will be worth it, right?" Matt said.

"I guess so," Ben said.

Again he didn't sound convinced. There was an expression Matt had heard from the NBA, about trusting the process when teams were rebuilding. He wanted Ben to trust this process, but wasn't sure that he did. Or would.

But it was like Matt had told him before:

At least he was here.

"You really believe this will help me get better?" Ben said.

Matt nodded.

"Easy for you to say," Ben said.

SEVEN

Sue Francis's office was in her home on the other side of South Shore.

"This feels like summer school," Matt said to his mom as they were driving over there.

"Have you ever complained about having to practice baseball?" Rachel Baker said.

"Mom," Matt said, "please don't compare speech therapy to baseball, okay?"

"Can if I want to," she said.

"What are you, twelve?" Matt said, grinning at her.

"You know what I say," she said to him. "Young once, immature forever."

"Working with Ms. Francis is *not* like playing baseball," Matt said.

"Wait a second," she said. "When you practice, isn't it about trying to become a better player?"

"Oh boy, here we go again," Matt said.

"Speech therapy is about helping you become better at speaking," she said.

"Baseball makes me happy," Matt said. "Therapy is a grind."

"But you *are* a grinder!" his mom said. "And getting the words out easier? That's going to make you happy too."

Matt had to admit.

She had him there.

Matt got stopped right away today, in his first few minutes in Ms. Francis's office, which really looked and felt more like the den where Matt watched baseball sometimes with his mom.

It hardly ever happened in here. He stuttered sometimes when he was with Ms. Francis, but not very often.

He was trying to tell her what he had worked on at Healey Park the day before, joking that he had felt like the therapist as he put Ben through a drill, and how hard it had been for his teammate.

"And who was this with?" she said

All he wanted to say was, "Ben Roberson."

But he couldn't. It was as if the *B* in "Ben" had closed his mouth and made it impossible to open.

He knew about all the drills they worked on in here. They talked about him "bouncing" to the next word he wanted to say or finding a different word. Ms. Francis had told him more than once, had told him a *lot,* to visualize water being stopped because of a knot in a hose, and picturing himself untying the knot.

But in the moment now, the same letter that was the first in Matt Baker's last name was tying him in a knot.

My own knot, he thought.

Except he couldn't even say "my."

It made him angry this time. He could feel his face reddening. He was finally able to say "My friend Ben," but as soon as he did, he pounded his fists on the side of his chair in frustration.

"I'll never be able to do this," he said.

"You sound like your friend," she said. "Are you going to let him give up?"

Matt shook his head.

"Well, I'll never let you give up," she said.

She smiled. He couldn't help himself and smiled back, then went slowly as he tried to explain all that to her as best he could. Without stopping.

"Well," Ms. Francis said when he finished, "that was certainly a mouthful."

"I'm sorry I got angry," he said.

"Don't be," she said. "Even anger is part of the process."

"Long one," Matt said.

"I keep telling you," she said, "think of it as a long season. Or even one game. You can strike out in the first inning, and still go on to play great, right?"

"I'm much better at playing a good game than talking a good game," Matt said.

Ms. Francis clapped her hands together.

"Let's do both," she said.

Matt still wanted to be outside. It was baseball weather again today. He wanted to be playing catch with José or Denzel or Kyle. He wouldn't even have minded being with Ben at Healey, as much of a grind as *their* session had been. He didn't want to have to wait for practice after dinner, he wanted to be on the field with his teammates right now.

But he was here. He was with Ms. Francis. She was trying to help him and he wanted her to help him. He knew she would never quit. He knew he would never quit. He wasn't wired that way.

He still wanted to be outside.

They were talking again about Matt identifying, or at least trying to identify, the times and the situations that made him stutter.

"It's weird," he said. "I know I struggle when I have to say something in front of the class. But at the same time, I can almost feel the kids in the class rooting for me. I get scared sometimes when I meet somebody who doesn't know I stutter. But I know my friends know."

He knew that had been another mouthful. But Matt had made it all the way through.

"Let's talk about that a little," she said. "You do find it happening with people you don't know. And who don't know that you stutter."

"Yes," he said.

"Do you ever think about telling people before it happens?" she said. "Putting it right there on the table?"

Matt shook his head quickly from side to side.

"No," he said. "I just hope it won't happen, so then people won't have to know."

"We've spoken about this plenty of times," she said. "You know this shouldn't make you feel badly about yourself, or think less of yourself. Or ashamed."

"I can't help it sometimes," Matt said.

"But you can help it," Sue Francis said, "and help yourself. I know enough about you by now to know that you refuse to let your lack of size hold you back in baseball. We're not going to let this hold you back."

"But it does," Matt said. "It *is*."

"It didn't hold George Springer back," she said.

Ms. Francis, who'd grown up outside of Houston, was an Astros fan, and proud of it.

"I wish I could beat stuttering the way he has," Matt said.

"He didn't beat anything," Ms. Francis said. "This isn't a game you win in the end with a big hit in the bottom of the last inning. This isn't about winning and losing. George Springer still stutters. But he has refused to let it beat *him*."

"I watched him during that World Series the Astros won," Matt said. "If you didn't know he stuttered, you wouldn't have known."

"Sure you would," she said. "He still stops, and slows down, and repeats words. He talks all the time about how he's just a normal person who happens to stutter. He says he just keeps trying to get better, the way he keeps getting better at baseball. And he sure was good enough at baseball to win that MVP award for the Series, wasn't he?"

"Yes," Matt said.

"George used to avoid public speaking as often as he could," she said. "And then during the World Series, with the whole world watching and all that media around, you couldn't shut the guy up."

"It took him a long time," Matt said.

"So what?" she said. "You think he was ready to be a World Series MVP when he was playing Little League?"

They did some of their exercises then. Ms. Francis asked him to describe—again—what his mouth felt like and what his throat felt like when he was unable to squeeze out a word. He told her that his throat would feel so tense sometimes he was afraid it might explode.

She had him close his eyes and imagine it was happening right then, even though it wasn't.

He did.

"Now pick a word, or a few words, and keep them going," she said. "Almost like you imagine a bubble bursting."

Matt smiled.

"Batter up," he said.

EIGHT

By batting practice that night, it was as if Ben Roberson had forgotten everything he and Matt had worked on the day before.

His swing looked exactly the same as it did before they had worked on making it shorter. He was swinging as hard as ever, and seemed to be having as much fun whether he connected or not.

Same guy, Matt thought, *different day*.

Matt wasn't going to say anything to him in front of their teammates. Maybe he wouldn't say anything at all unless Ben brought it up. But as he watch him cut and miss or occasionally hit what Sarge called one of his "big flies," Matt couldn't help think he'd wasted his time *trying* to help him.

Ben either didn't want to put in the work and the time required to become a more disciplined hitter, or in the course of one day he had managed to unlearn everything. Maybe he'd just been going through the motions when there was no audience around, and nobody to go crazy when he did manage to hit one deep.

Maybe he was afraid of looking bad.

One of the last balls Ben hit in batting practice was a weak grounder to José's side of second base. Matt had been moving toward the ball himself, but pulled up when he saw it was much closer to José, then waited at second base as José flipped the ball to him, as if they were about to start a double play.

They were both standing there as Ben managed to send one of those big flies over the wall in dead center on his last batting practice swing.

"He sure is fun to watch," José said to Matt.

"What's the Spanish word that means to mash?" Matt said.

José grinned. "Mash!" he said.

"Ben sure can mash," Matt said.

"He's something," José said.

"Yeah," Matt said. "Isn't he?"

He left it at that. Kyle Sargent was batting now, then Matt would go after him. When it was Matt's turn, he knew what to expect from Sarge's pitches by now. He wasn't just going to try to throw them over the middle of the plate. He wanted Matt to think, and he wanted him to work. So he worked him inside, and Matt would try to pull the ball. He worked him away, to see if Matt could go with the pitch to right. He threw balls too high, to see if Matt would lay off them. Or in the dirt. Matt knew Sarge didn't do this with all the other players. He did it with Kyle and Denzel, Matt knew. The rest of the guys he would just groove pitches, as a way of helping them with their confidence.

But he wanted to challenge Matt, every single day. And when he did groove one to Matt, threw him what Sarge liked to joke was a "crush me" fastball, he expected Matt to give it a ride.

He did that with his second-to-last swing of the night, hitting one high up the wall in right-center and nearly getting it out. Maybe there was a part of him that wanted to put on a BP show of his own tonight, show Ben what hitting looked like when you did it right. So he did.

The last pitch Sarge threw him was at the knees and on the outside corner. Matt kept his weight back and his head on it

MIKE LUPICA

and might have hit the ball as hard as the one that had nearly been a home run. Ben was at first, and it was a good thing he was paying attention or the screamer might have caught him in the middle of his chest. Ben, who had good footwork, had time to step to the side, backhand the ball, and toss it back to Sarge.

"Okay," Ben yelled at Matt, grinning. "That hurt. Bigly."

They took a water break after that, before Sarge would run them through some game situations in the field, even putting some guys on the bases.

"Talk to you for a second?" Ben said.

"Sure," Matt said.

Ben led him out behind first base.

"Hey," Ben said, trying to keep his voice low. "I know I wasn't swinging tonight the way you want me to."

All Matt wanted to do was tell him that was okay. But he couldn't get out that word: "Okay." When he tried, it sounded a little bit as if he were choking on something.

As frustrated as he was, Ben seemed even more frustrated. He was also unwilling to wait for Matt to get the word out. But he seemed to know exactly what Matt was trying to say because he barreled in and said, "It's not okay!"

Matt saw some of their teammates turn around, because what Ben had just said, he'd said in a loud voice.

But there was nothing Matt could do right now. Ben didn't

seem to mind, and kept right on going. At least he lowered his voice.

"I was just afraid that if I tried all that stuff in front of the other guys tonight I'd look like an idiot," Ben said.

The best Matt could do was nod, and drink more water. Now there was no point in saying anything at all.

Then Sarge was telling them to get back on the field, they only had about fifteen minutes left to practice, it was time to put the bats down to work on fielding and baserunning.

"Anybody can swing and miss," Sarge said. "That's just a physical mistake. But what our team isn't going to do is make mistakes running the bases, or throwing to the right base."

There were twelve players on their team, and Sarge had promised that everybody was going to get their fair amount of playing time. But having the extra guys meant he could put two runners on the bases. And for those last fifteen minutes of practice, he hit ground balls and fly balls, telling them there was one out or two outs, even telling them that they were up a run or down a run or tied. He made the outfielders hit the cut-off man on balls he'd hit out there. If they didn't hit the cut-off man, he made everybody start all over again.

Every once in a while, when everything worked the way Sarge wanted it to, he'd stop and tell them again that what they were doing might not feel like it, but it was all part of the beauty of baseball, even if it felt like grunt work.

"You see what I'm talking about more when you're at a game than when you're watching on television," Sarge said. "As soon as a ball is put in play, if the team in the field is on top of things, everybody out there is in motion. If they're not, they're the ones who should be watching the game instead of playing it."

Now the Astros were the ones in motion, making sure they were in the right spot, making the right throws.

Sarge was right.

It *was* a beautiful game.

The first game of their season was on Friday night. Matt was sure they were all ready for it. And no one was more ready than he was.

Neither Ben's parents nor Matt's mom were in the parking lot when practice ended. So the two of them grabbed their water bottles and just sat on the infield grass, between first base and the pitcher's mound.

Matt could tell Ben still wanted to talk about it, even if Matt didn't.

"It's like I was trying to tell you before," Ben said. "Maybe this isn't the time to be messing with my swing, with the season about to start."

That made no sense. But Matt let it go. It had been a long

day, first his session with Ms. Francis and now what had been a good, long practice.

"Okay," Matt said.

"I talked to my dad about it last night," Ben said. "He just told me to be myself."

"Okay," Matt said again.

He looked over Ben's shoulder and saw his mom pulling up, leaning out the window and waving at him, a big smile on her face. Matt wasn't just happy to see her. He was almost relieved.

Ben said, "My dad said he'd trade a few strikeouts for one long ball any day of the week. He said that's what everybody's doing in the big leagues now."

There was no point in telling him that they weren't *in* the big leagues. It was another thought he kept inside him, this time voluntarily.

"You have to be yourself," Matt said.

"Maybe I can't be you and you can't be me," Ben said.

Matt stood up then, put out his fist so Ben could pound him.

"Good talk," he said, even though he knew it hadn't been.

Even though he felt like yet again tonight, Ben had swung and missed.

MIKE LUPICA

NINE

After a late dinner, Matt went into the den to watch a game on the MLB Network, the Orioles against the Yankees. A second baseman he really liked was playing, Jonathan Schoop of the Orioles. Schoop could really hit and field his position. He was one of those players who made the hard plays look easy and never went out of his way to make the easy plays look hard just to draw attention to himself.

"You don't root for either one of those teams," Matt's mom

said after they'd cleaned up in the kitchen. "So why is this game such a big deal?"

"Mom, it's baseball and it's on. It's practically my duty to watch," he said. "You want to join me?"

"Not tonight," she said, and then told him she was heading upstairs to watch some new series on Netflix.

"Everybody in it must speak with English accents," Matt said.

"Of course," she said. Then she grinned at him. "It's set in England and it's on. It's practically my duty to watch."

Matt settled in on the couch to watch the game. He was still thinking about what Sarge had said about the beauty of baseball and everybody being in motion. Matt hated it when people talked about how boring baseball was.

On the screen in front of him, almost on cue, Schoop went behind second base to backhand a ball that looked like a single all the way coming off the bat of Aaron Judge. He effortlessly flipped the ball out of his glove to the Orioles shortstop, who glided across second base and started a 4-6-3 double play, ending the half inning for the Yankees.

"Wow," Matt said out loud.

"Talking to yourself, or the game?" he heard his mom say.

He hadn't even noticed her standing in the doorway.

"Both," he said. "What about Netflix?"

"It can wait," she said. "Decided to watch a little baseball with my boy after all."

He knew his mom honestly did love baseball, from the time she had been a star softball player herself.

After the commercial, Schoop was leading off for the Orioles, and hit the first pitch he saw, one that looked to be off the plate, into the right field corner past Judge for a double.

"Look at him going with the pitch," his mom said.

"You really do know a lot about baseball," Matt said, grinning. "For a girl."

She punched him lightly in the arm.

"Good thing I know you're kidding," she said. "I mean, you have a decent sense of humor. For a boy."

"Good one, Mom," he said, then told her about how he'd gone with an outside pitch at practice and nearly tore the glove off Ben's hand.

"I forgot to ask," his mom said. "How did it work out tonight with Ben's new swing?"

"Didn't," Matt said.

"Well, it will take him some time."

"He didn't even try," Matt said. "He just went back to his usual way of doing it."

"Did he explain why?"

"Yeah, he did," Matt said. "He said his dad wants him to be a home run hitter."

"Is that what Ben wants?" she said.

"Doesn't seem to matter," Matt said. "He said that guys in the big leagues are willing to trade three strikeouts for one home run, and if it's good enough for them, it should be good enough for Ben."

Matt's mom picked up the remote and muted the TV.

"If his dad doesn't want him to change the way he does things," she said, "it's gonna be kind of hard for Ben to do it on his own."

"But he can do it if he wants to," Matt said.

"How much does he want to?"

"He really listens to his dad," Matt said.

"Not so terrible, listening to your parents," his mom said. "Unless one of them is giving out bad advice."

"You never give me bad advice," Matt said to her.

"Hope not."

"You always tell me to be myself," Matt said.

"If you ever stop, you're grounded," she joked.

A few minutes later Schoop did it again, this time going to his left and into short right field, making a sliding stop, somehow side-arming the ball to Chris Davis while his momentum was still carrying him toward his own right fielder. Didi

Gregorius, the Yankees shortstop, was out by a step. Schoop jogged off the field as if what he'd done was strictly routine, instead of completely spectacular. The only show of emotion from him was when he tapped Davis's glove as the two of them went down the dugout steps.

My kind of player, Matt thought.

"That was baseball," his mom said.

"Totally," Matt said. He smiled at her and said, "Even with the sound off."

Then he said, "Mom, you don't have to stay with me. Go watch your show."

"If you say so," she said, trying to sound as if she were the one with the British accent.

It was a fast game, and Matt was able to watch it all the way to the end. He wasn't one of those people who wanted clocks on the field. He loved the idea that you *couldn't* run out the clock in a baseball game. He just wanted pitchers to stop stepping off the rubber after every pitch. He wanted batters to stay in the batter's box. He loved that they had changed the rules and there were only so many visits catchers and coaches and managers could make to the mound during a game.

He didn't want them to change everything. He just wanted them to pick up the pace a little.

When he went upstairs to say good night to his mom, she said, "You stressing on this thing with Ben?"

"Maybe there's nothing I can do," Matt said, "if his dad wants him to be one kind of hitter, even if Ben wants to be another kind."

"Would be kind of a problem."

"I just want to help our team," Matt said.

"You can only control what you can control," she said. "And if Ben really wants your help, you just have to trust that he'll ask for it again."

She was already in bed, but got out now and hugged him. She was a major hugger, his mom. But Matt was too. There were things in his life that scared him. He knew the fear that came over him when the words wouldn't come out. But he had never been afraid to show affection with his mom. He couldn't even remember now if he'd ever been the same way with his dad.

"It's not like I'm the coach of the team," Matt said to her.

"You sure about that?" Rachel Baker said.

TEN

First game of the season.

No matter how young or old you were, Matt knew, your own opening day—or night—*never* got old.

He'd been excited when the Nationals played their first game in the spring, on this same field at Healey Park. But this felt even better, just because it was All-Stars, and you knew the level of competition was about to get better. It was all the best players in your town against the best players from somebody else's town, all summer long.

Their opponent tonight was the Lake Worth Cubs. Lake Worth was about forty minutes from South Shore. Matt remembered some of their players from last year, but not all of them. One guy he did remember was the Cubs starting pitcher, a tall right-hander named Andrew Welles. He had been one of the biggest players in last summer's league, and had thrown harder than anybody Matt had faced. He looked even bigger now. Matt was guessing that the speed of his fastball had grown right along with him.

"If they're on All-Stars, they all must be good," Kyle Sargent was saying before the Astros got ready to take the field for infield practice.

"So are we," José Dominguez said.

"So let's get this party started," Denzel Lincoln said.

They all looked at him, shaking their heads and smiling.

"Did you really just say that?" Matt said.

"Hey," Denzel said, "I'm feeling it, okay?"

The top of the batting order was just as Sarge had told them it would be: Kyle, followed by José, followed by Matt, followed by Ben, then Stone Russell, all the way to Denzel, who Sarge said was like another leadoff man at the bottom of the order.

Andrew Welles was warming up behind his team's bench,

on their side of Healey, while Matt and José stood near second base waiting for Sarge to start hitting ground balls.

"He looks as strong as Justin Verlander," Matt said.

"No worries," José said. "You can hit him."

Matt had had a little success against Andrew Welles last summer, but not a lot.

"And you know this . . . *how?*"

"Because you can hit anybody," José said, and put up his glove so Matt could slap it with his own.

They fielded some ground balls. They made some throws to Ben at first base. Stone Russell threw down to second from home plate with his great arm. José took the throw. He flipped the ball to Matt. They ran off the field, ready to play the Cubs and start the season.

Everything felt new tonight. The baselines looked as white as they could possibly look. The grass shouldn't have looked any different than it did from their last practice, but somehow it did. Somehow it looked greener. *It is all good*, Matt thought. If you got a hit your first time up, you were batting 1.000. If you made an out your next time up, your average was still .500.

Matt sat on the end of the Astros' bench and looked out at the bright white lines and the green grass and imagined a whole summer stretching out in front of him and his teammates, all the way to the finals of the state tournament if they made it that far. That would mean a game in the new stadium at the state university. To Matt, it felt as if they were trying to play their way to Yankee Stadium.

Before the Astros starting pitcher, Teddy Sample, got ready to throw his first pitches in the top of the first, Sarge gathered the Astros around him in the small grassy area between their bench and the wire fence that separated the field from the bleachers, where his mom sat. Matt gave a quick wave to her. He saw Ben's dad, Bob, sitting a couple of rows behind them. Bob, Matt knew, was at least six-five. Even sitting down, he seemed to tower over everyone around him.

Sarge was smiling. But then Sarge seemed to be smiling every time he stepped out on this field, whether it was for a practice or the first game of the season. Kyle said that usually his dad was more impatient to get to Healey Park than he was.

"The guys who played for me in the spring have heard me talk about this before," Sarge said now. "And what they've heard me say is that I just wasn't smart enough to know how good I had it when I was your age. I thought I knew how great nights like this were. But they were even better than that."

Some of the Astros were turned around on the bench, facing away from the field. The rest were standing. Sarge was leaning against the wire fence, still with the bat he'd used to hit grounders during infield practice in his hand.

"But since kids now are *way* smarter than they were when I was your age, I know you guys are smart enough to appreciate the journey we're about to start," he said. "And I know you're all going to appreciate the heck out of competing."

He walked up so he was closer to them, and lowered his voice.

"Kyle's mom asked me the other day if coaching gave me the same feeling that playing baseball used to give me," Sarge said. "And I told her, *Heck no!* But this isn't about me. This is your game now. So let's go play it. Would that be okay with you guys?"

They all yelled *"Yes!"* in one voice. Matt felt as if his was the loudest. In that moment if Sarge had asked him to jump over the screen behind home plate to play this game, he was pretty sure he could have done it.

Sarge had talked about playing the season.

It was even simpler than that, Matt Baker thought.

Play. Ball.

Teddy Sample struck out the first two batters he faced. Andrew Welles was hitting third for them. Even though Andrew threw right-handed he batted left, and could really hit. He wasn't a power hitter the way Ben was. Didn't hit those big flies. He had a beautiful, level swing made for line drives.

Now he put a great swing on the third pitch he saw from Teddy, on the inside half of the plate, and ripped a shot between Matt and Ben. Ben didn't react quickly enough to the ball, and had no chance at it.

Matt did.

He read the ball perfectly off Andrew's bat and didn't try to cut the ball off as he moved to his left, knowing it would be past him too. So he headed for the outfield grass. When he got there, he dove for the ball, making sure to keep his glove down, not wanting to have timed his play just right and have the ball skip over his glove.

At the end of his dive he got that thrill you got on a play like this, because he could feel the ball in his glove.

Now it was just all instinct. All baseball. The ball had been hit hard enough that he knew he had time. Not a lot of time. Some. He scrambled to his knees and made a strong, sidearm throw to Ben, who made a full stretch, his own body angled toward the outfield.

They got Andrew Welles by a step.

Matt was still on his knees in short right field when he saw the first base umpire signal that Andrew was out. Then he got up, kept his head down, ran off the field. He didn't even tap gloves with Ben as he ran alongside him. No celebration. No big deal. It was still just the top of the first.

MIKE LUPICA

Kyle walked to lead off the Astros' half of the first. José struck out on a high fastball from Andrew Welles, ball up in his eyes on a 3-2 count. He couldn't lay off. Had no chance to do anything except wave at it. Strike three.

As he walked back to the bench, he passed Matt, leaned close, and said, "You know how hard we thought he threw? He throws *way* harder than that."

As Matt dug in, he tapped the shin guards of the Cubs catcher, Jake McAuliffe, another kid he remembered from last year's Lake Worth team.

"Go easy on us," Jake said.

"No can do," is what Matt wanted to say.

The words wouldn't come out.

His jaw just locked up on him. But he couldn't worry about that right now. He was only worrying about Andrew Welles, and focusing on that fastball.

So he just shook his head at Jake, as if that's all he wanted to say.

He bought himself another second by reaching down and using his bat to knock dirt out of his spike. Then he turned to face Andrew Welles, telling himself to forget about everything else except the pitcher.

So far he had thrown every pitch as hard as he could, and did that now with Matt, throwing one that came in about shoulder high. Maybe it would have been a strike to Kyle or José. Ball one. When Jake threw the ball back to Andrew, Andrew snapped his glove at the ball, almost swiping it out of the air, as if it had only taken one pitch for Matt's small strike zone to annoy him.

The second pitch came in just as hard, was way inside, and backed Matt off the plate. Ball two. Matt had never been afraid of the ball, even when it was being thrown this hard, by somebody this much bigger than he was. But he didn't want to take one off the knee or in the ribs, either.

"The big dude is kind of scary, isn't he?" Jake said through his mask.

This time the words came right out.

"Not to me," Matt said quietly.

The count was 2-0. But Matt knew that Andrew could see Ben waiting in the on-deck circle. He had to be thinking he'd rather have Ben lead off the bottom of the second than come up with Matt on base with a walk. Matt thought: *If he doesn't want to walk me, this might be the best pitch I'm going to see.* Sometimes you only got one in an at bat.

He didn't know why he thought Andrew might come inside again, but he did.

And Andrew did.

And Matt was ready.

MIKE LUPICA

It probably would have been a strike if Matt had taken it. But he didn't take it. Maybe the fastball pitcher had forgotten from one season to the next how fast Matt's bat speed was. He was all over the pitch, covering it easily, lining it over the third baseman's head and all the way into the left field corner. By the time the ball was back to the infield, Matt was standing on second base with a double, and his first hit of the season, and Kyle was on third.

Now it was their scary dude, Ben, against the Cubs scary dude, second and third, one out.

All they needed to get a run was for Ben to put the ball in play. It was too early in the game for the Cubs to bring their infielders in. They were playing at normal depth. So even a ground ball would score a run. If it got through the infield, the Astros would get two.

Matt found himself looking over at the Cubs third baseman, knowing what it was like to have Ben Roberson standing there just sixty feet away. It had happened to Matt plenty of times when he'd been a baserunner on third. Because of Ben's size and reach, it looked as if he could practically reach out and tap you on the helmet with his bat if he wanted to.

It was only the bottom of the first, first game of the season. It still felt like a big moment.

Until it wasn't.

Andrew struck out Ben on three pitches. It was like the announcers said sometimes: Good morning, good afternoon, good night. Ben wasn't trying to just put the ball in play. He was trying to hit a three-run homer off Andrew Welles, and struck out on three straight fastballs instead. But Stone Russell did much better, blooping a two-strike pitch into center, not trying to do too much with it, just trying to get his bat on the ball. With two outs, Matt was running all the way, and scored easily. Astros 2, Cubs 0.

When Matt was back on the bench, having been high-fived by his teammates, Ben said, "I know what you're thinking."

"That I'm happy we've got a two-run lead?"

"That I shouldn't have been swinging out of my shoes like that," Ben said.

"Nope," Matt said. "All I'm really thinking is that you've seen Andrew now and you'll get him next time."

The game stayed at 2–0 until the bottom of the third. This time José worked Andrew for a walk. So did Matt. Runners on first and second. It meant two more guys on the bases for Ben.

"*Give it a ride, big boy!*"

It was the only voice you could hear at Healey Park, and Matt knew instantly that it belonged to Ben's dad.

"*Take him deep!*"

And Ben nearly did. But what looked for a second as if it

might actually be a three-run homer turned into a routine out for the left fielder, even if it had been a really, really *high* routine out to end the inning.

Ben walked back to the bench, looking up to the stands, where his dad was standing and pumping a fist at him, as if just giving the ball a ride had been enough.

Enough to do everything except get the Astros another run.

Everything except that.

ELEVEN

The game was tied 2–2 going into the fifth inning. Teddy Sample hadn't reached the maximum number of pitches Sarge allowed his starters to throw. But as far as Sarge was concerned, Teddy was close enough. So he brought Chris Conte in from left field to relieve Teddy, and maybe close out the game if the Astros could scratch out at least one run.

But it was the Cubs who broke the tie, scoring three runs in the top of the fifth to go ahead 5–2. Two of those runs came on a monster home run by Andrew Welles, who by now had moved over to play third base. It was what Sarge called a "no-doubter." Teddy had gone out to replace Chris in left and had only taken one step back before simply doing what everybody else in Healey Park was doing:

Watching Andrew's ball disappear over the fence.

The Astros did nothing in the bottom of the inning with the reliever the Cubs brought in to replace Andrew, a small left-hander—though not as small as Matt—whom Matt didn't recognize from last season. Chris got the Cubs out in order in the top of the sixth. Last ups now for the Astros in their opener, down three runs, three outs left.

The Cubs left-hander got two quick outs, and it looked as if the Astros were about to go quietly in the bottom of the sixth, as quiet as their bench area had become.

Matt was his team's last chance. Before he left the on-deck circle he gave a quick turn and looked up to where all the parents were seated in the bleachers, and saw his great baseball mom mouth two words:

Get on.

In that moment, Matt Baker felt the way he used to when he was playing in the small park down the street from his house, when he knew he and his friends were getting close to suppertime.

He didn't want to stop playing yet.

Sometimes baseball, even in All-Stars, was as simple and pure as that.

He needed to get on. Somehow.

The Cubs catcher didn't say anything as Matt got into the batter's box. There was some mild chatter from the infield.

"You got this, Robbie."

"One more out."

"All you, baby."

Matt took a look around at the defense as he dug in. He always wondered which guys in the field really wanted the ball hit to them at the end of a game, and which ones didn't. Because Matt knew that not all of them did.

I'm not making the last out, he told himself.

He couldn't think of a single time during the spring season when he'd been the one to make the last out of a game, and he wasn't planning to start now.

He couldn't win the game right here.

Just keep it going.

The left-hander, Robbie, threw Matt two pretty good fast-balls, one high, both with what Sarge liked to call giddy-up on them. But it wasn't the kind of heat Andrew had thrown.

Wait for your pitch.

It turned out to be the next pitch, a fastball down the middle.

MIKE LUPICA

Matt jumped on it, lining the ball past Robbie before he could even get his glove up and on into center field. Matt hadn't made the last out. The Astros were still playing. When he got to first base, he gave a good, hard slap to the side of his leg.

Yeah.

Heck, yeah.

Big Ben walked to the plate.

Matt watched him from first base as he smiled and said something to the Cubs catcher. Matt couldn't hear what it was. He just didn't want him to be thinking about hitting a home run here, because all that would do was make it a 5–4 game, the Astros still down a run, nobody on base.

Matt just wanted Ben to keep the line moving, give Stone a chance to come to the plate as the potential tying run.

Or give Stone a chance to keep the line moving.

And let them all keep playing.

Matt looked over at Robbie, the Cubs pitcher. He saw how big Robbie's eyes were as Big Ben got himself ready, hands set high, bat still, the way the rest of him was still as he looked out at the pitcher.

Then Matt heard it, because everybody at Healey did:

"All you!"

Matt didn't even have to turn around. He knew it was Ben's dad. By now, everybody knew that voice.

"All you, big man!"

The familiar voice was telling Ben to try to go deep. Ball one was so far outside that the Cubs catcher had to lunge for it to keep Matt from advancing to second base on the wild pitch. Ball two was in the dirt.

He doesn't want to pitch to him, Matt realized.

This was good. This was very good. If Robbie continued to be this wild, there was no chance that Ben was going to swing. Robbie would end up walking him. It would be first and second. Stone would represent the tying run.

Ball three was so high that the Cubs catcher had to jump out of his crouch to keep another pitch from skipping back to the screen behind the plate.

Take the walk.

Matt wanted his voice to go right into Ben's brain. *Take the walk. Keep the line moving.* Stone Russell wasn't just a solid hitter with power. He knew the strike zone so well for somebody their age, maybe because he looked at it all game long as catcher. He made you throw him strikes, and once he did get strikes, he knew what to do with them. Matt remembered how many balls in the gap he'd hit in the spring, when he was playing for the Angels. Nobody on Matt's team had *ever* wanted to see him up in a big spot.

Take the walk!

It was as if Matt's brain were trying to scream its way into Ben's now.

Take the pitch, take the walk.

Right now Robbie had a better chance of turning into a real astro, as in astronaut, than he did of throwing a strike to Ben.

He didn't. The fourth pitch wasn't as high as the third pitch had been. Close enough. A fastball that was up in Ben's eyes. Ball four easy.

Except it wasn't.

Ben swung at it, even though Sarge had been clear from the first night of practice that no one was to swing at a 3-0 pitch unless Sarge gave the green light. Matt had watched Sarge go through his signs in the third-base coach's box. Not only had he not given Ben the green light. The only sign he'd given was the "take" sign. Repeatedly.

Ben just barely managed to get his bat on the ball, way up near the end of the bat, and popped weakly to Andrew Welles at third.

Third out.

Game over.

The Astros were 0–1.

Matt had been running all the way as soon as Ben made contact, because there were two outs. But he'd only made it as far as second base by the time the ball ended up in Andrew's glove. When he stopped, he saw Ben make the right turn before he got to first base, already walking back to the bench. Stone Russell was still standing in the on-deck circle.

Sarge was still in the coaching box, arms crossed in front of him, staring at Ben, his eyes following Ben all the way back to the Astros' bench.

Matt stood on second base.

"Take the walk," he said, only loud enough for himself to hear.

The words came out of him just fine.

TWELVE

Knowing Sarge, and the kind of person he was and the kind of coach he was, Matt didn't expect him to pull Ben aside for swinging away on 3-0.

He wouldn't say what he was going to say in front of the team, either. That wasn't Sarge's way. One of his big things was that no one on the Astros was ever to show up the other team. Matt had never seen Sarge show up anybody on his own team.

But there was going to be a conversation, and soon, Matt

was sure of that. Ben hadn't just missed a sign. He *ignored* the sign, and ignored a team rule in the process. And it was worse than that. Ben had missed the *point.* It was almost as if he had decided he was going to hit a three-run homer and tie the game, even though there was only one man on base. What he wanted to do, or maybe what Ben's dad wanted him to do in that moment, was more important than what his team *needed* him to do.

As Matt was walking toward the parking lot with his mom, he saw Ben and his dad well ahead of them. Ben's dad had his arm around his son's shoulder.

They were laughing.

Then Ben's dad stopped, as if holding a bat in his hand, and took a huge uppercut swing. After his follow-through, he laughed again and pointed to the sky as if he were following the path of an imaginary home run, before the two of them got into his convertible and drove away.

Matt's mom was watching Matt watch them.

"It's only one game," she said.

Her hand was on Matt's shoulder now.

"I know," Matt said. "Doesn't make it hurt any less."

"And I know you're all about playing the game right, all the way to the final out," Rachel Baker said. "We *both* know Ben didn't do that tonight."

There was so much Matt wanted to say, if only for his mom. He wanted to say that everybody ought to play the game right. It wasn't about making a play in the field or making an error, getting a hit or striking out. Playing the game right was about being in the right place, making the right decision. And always—*always*—putting the team first.

But there was no point, no matter how badly Ben had missed the point.

That wasn't the worst part.

The worst part was that he couldn't say anything right now even if he wanted to. He could feel himself locking up, or locking down, and becoming even more frustrated. His mouth wouldn't work, his tongue wouldn't work. Matt could even feel his back tightening up the way it did. He couldn't take in any air.

A long night got longer.

The best he could so was start shaking his head, slowly at first, then faster and faster.

His mom squeezed his shoulder.

"I hear you," she said. "I hear you."

THIRTEEN

Matt was alone in his room later that night, door closed, watching a baseball game on his laptop, Cubs against the Brewers, focusing most on the middle infielders, as usual.

Tonight he paid particularly close attention to Javier Baez, the Cubs second baseman. He knew people hadn't been talking as much about Baez as they had the year the Cubs had finally won the World Series after 108 years. But Matt hadn't forgotten him. He knew how talented Baez was, particularly in the field.

And Matt was doing something else while he watched:

He was reading the rosters of all the major league teams. Aloud. He kept his voice down. He didn't want his mom to hear him. But he was reading one name after another, even the ones he knew he might not be pronouncing correctly. Sometimes he would do it by division, starting with the American League East, then going to the Central, and the West. Like that. Sometimes he would just randomly jump around from team to team. It wasn't that he was trying to memorize all the players on all the teams.

He just wanted to make it through all the players without stuttering one time.

Sometimes, when he got to the last couple of teams, he'd actually feel as if he'd put some pressure on himself, having challenged himself again to make it all the way through all thirty teams. But if he did power through, he wouldn't just feel as if he'd won something.

He'd feel fluent.

It was one of Ms. Francis's favorite words.

Fluent.

As if all those names flowed out of him, off his lips, out into the air.

He did that tonight, all the way through the National League West. He spoke in his quiet but fluent voice. Not his stuttering voice. Not the one he hated.

In that moment, he felt as if he were a different person: Fluent Matt Baker.

So now the same guy who had even stuttered in front of his mom after tonight's game had just ripped through the roster of the San Diego Padres. He'd made it through all thirty teams.

Yeah, he thought to himself.

Same guy.

The guy he wanted to be.

On his laptop screen Kris Bryant, the Cubs third baseman, made a backhand stop behind the base, and then threw a strike across the diamond to Anthony Rizzo.

Matt turned himself into a play-by-play man, still keeping his voice low.

"Great stop by Bryant," he said to himself. "And an even better throw across to Rizzo!"

Ms. Francis had cautioned him not to think of things in terms of "winning" and "losing," because when he did get stopped, when he did stutter, that didn't make him a loser. Nobody was keeping score on him.

Matt hadn't rushed. Nobody had a clock on him. AL East, AL Central, AL West, NL East, NL Central, NL West. He did feel some pressure when he got to the Padres.

Powered through.

At least he'd won something tonight.

You really did have to take your small victories where you found them.

FOURTEEN

Healey Park was a big place—a big, happy place. Matt had always thought of it as the center of life in South Shore. There were the two Little League fields, a playground, a half-dozen clay tennis courts, even a duck pond. There was a narrow road that cut through the center of the park, not for cars, just for bikes, and on the other side of the road was the big field where South Shore High played its home games, and where Babe Ruth All-Stars played in the summer.

Matt and José Dominguez were on the back Little League field after lunch for the two-man practice they'd scheduled the night before by text. They'd each brought a bat. Matt had brought an bag of old balls that he and his mom used so that he and José could pitch to each other. For now, though, they were just working on fielding. Matt would stand on first base and throw ground balls to José at short. Then they'd switch off, and Matt would take his place at second, and José would throw him ground balls. Sometimes Matt would cheat toward the base, José would throw him a grounder, Matt would move to his right and step on second and then make his throw, as if trying to complete a double play.

Sometimes Matt would go over to short and make the throw from there, just for the fun of it.

"How am I gonna make that throw next season when we're the ones playing on the big field?" José said.

"You'll be bigger and your arm will be stronger," Matt said.

He thought: *Hope I'm bigger by next year.*

"Not strong enough!" José said.

"But remember something," Matt said. "The runners will have farther to run to get to first base next year. So you'll have more time than you think."

José grinned. "Are you ever *not* thinking about baseball?" he said.

"Sure," Matt said. "Sometimes I think about ice cream."

"Not until we finish our practice!" José said.

"What are you, my coach?" Matt said.

Matt had thought about inviting Ben to join them, but had decided against it. It wasn't because of the way the Cubs game had ended. He honestly wasn't angry with Ben about that. He still liked Ben. And the more Matt saw Ben's dad—and listened to Ben's dad—the more he could see and hear what kind of hitter his dad wanted him to be. Matt knew that he and Ben were just plain different. So he had to live with the fact that Ben wasn't ever going to take baseball as seriously as Matt did.

He wasn't going to take losing as hard, or not show it if he did.

So he'd just decided to make this a Ben-free day with José, who did love baseball the way Matt did, and who never seemed to want to come off the field, even today, when it was just the two of them.

They took a break finally and sat in the grass and drank from their water bottles.

"I can't wait for our next game," José said.

It would be against the Glenallen Giants on Tuesday night.

"Same," Matt said. "You know what makes me jealous about players in the big leagues? They get to play practically every day."

"I hear you," José said. "If they have a tough loss like we just had, they can make it disappear the next day or night."

"They're lucky," Matt said.

José smiled, and put out a fist for Matt to bump.

"It's not so terrible being us, either," José said.

He stood up.

"Let's hit," he said.

They both hit for a while, collected the balls, then hit a little more. They decided that before they called it a day, they both wanted to field more ground balls. José got the last one. Matt didn't make it easy for him, throwing a hard grounder to his right, making him backhand the ball as he moved toward third base. But somehow José stopped himself, twisted his body just enough and snapped off a sweet throw to Matt at first.

"*Buen tiro!*" Matt yelled.

It meant "good throw" in Spanish.

"Wow," José said. "You really have been studying."

They met at the pitcher's mound.

"Still kind of working on English myself," Matt said.

By now José was as patient about the stuttering as most of Matt's friends were. Not all. But most. They hadn't been teammates for very long, but there hadn't been one time when José had finished one of Matt's sentences when he'd gotten stuck, or blocked.

"We'll keep helping each other," José said now.

They touched gloves.

"Todo bien," Matt said, grinning.

All good.

Something else that was good: Because school was out and it was summer now, there was an ice cream truck parked near the duck pond every day. Matt and José had both brought money with them and walked over to the truck now, gloves hung over their bats, bats on their shoulders. It was just one of those summer days that you wanted to last forever, the way you wanted summer to.

There was a line of kids and parents in front of them, starting from the ice cream truck's window.

Matt stopped.

"You know," he said to José, "I'm not feeling it on ice cream all of a sudden."

"Are you serious, *compadre*?" José said. "The only thing I've been thinking about since we got to this park, other than baseball, is a double scoop of chocolate, sugar cone, with sprinkles."

Matt could feel his throat getting dry and his heart starting to beat a little rapidly. He heard Ms. Francis's voice inside his head, telling him not to project, which was her way of telling him not to anticipate trouble before it happened.

He thought: *It's been such a good day.*

MIKE LUPICA

"Okay," Matt said, and took his place at the back of the line with José.

Maybe he wasn't projecting. Maybe he was just being plain silly.

There were a couple of girls Matt didn't know, about his age, right behind him and José, talking away, laughing, checking their phones, taking pictures of each other, checking the pictures, all the while discussing whether they wanted a cone or a cup.

Matt wasn't saying anything. He could feel himself beginning to tighten up, not just his throat and mouth, but his whole body. Usually people hated being in long, slow lines like this one. Not Matt. Not right now. He even thought about telling José to just get him a strawberry cone, two scoops, and that he wanted to go use the rest room. Or that he'd go find them a table. Anything.

But that would be taking the easy way out. Maybe what he was feeling would pass. Maybe he could power through. He looked over his shoulder. The line behind him, and behind the girls, was as long as the line in front of them.

Matt took some deep breaths.

At least he was getting air in.

Words starting with s could be the hardest sometimes.

"Strawberry," Matt said.

Practicing.

"What?" José said.

"Gonna get strawberry," Matt said.

So far, so good.

Finally they got to the front of the line. Another deep breath for Matt. The kid in the window had one of those little three-cornered hats. He looked like he was in high school. He was smiling.

"What can I get for you guys?" he said.

José gave him his order.

The kid in the window turned his attention to Matt.

"What about you, little dude?" he said.

Then it was happening to Matt the way he knew it was going to happen, as soon as he'd seen the line.

"S-s-s" was all that came out of his mouth, sounding like his breath.

Nothing but air.

José knew what was happening as soon as Matt didn't make his order. Maybe he wanted to jump in. He knew what kind of ice cream Matt wanted. But José did not jump in. He knew better. He was playing by Matt's rules, even though Matt wanted him to break the rules in that moment.

The kid in the window was still smiling.

"Can't make up your mind?" he said finally, glancing past Matt at the line behind him.

Matt swallowed.

"S-s-s."

He did not want to be here. He wanted to walk away. Or run away. All these strangers, waiting on him now.

"Come *on*," he heard one of the girls behind him say.

"We're *waiting*," the girl with her said.

Matt could hear himself making his order.

Only inside his head.

"Is there a *problem*?" the first girl said.

She had no idea.

"Chocolate," Matt Baker finally said.

He heard one of the girls behind him—he didn't know which one, no way he was turning around—sigh loudly.

"One scoop or two," the kid in the window said.

Matt held up two fingers.

The kid made the two cones, one with sprinkles, one without. Matt didn't even like chocolate ice cream that much. It didn't matter. The kid in the window told him how much for the two cones. Matt told José he'd pay for both. He'd brought enough money. José said he didn't have to do that.

"Yeah," Matt said, "I do."

The two of them walked away with their cones, back toward the field, stopping to sit down under a tree in the shade.

"Sorry," Matt said.

It was an *s* word that came right out of him.

José smiled and told him there was no need to apologize, he'd just gotten a free ice cream cone out of this deal.

"It just happens," Matt said.

His breathing was back to normal. His speech was back to normal. Even if he wasn't.

José was still smiling. There was chocolate ice cream all over his mouth.

"We're a team, remember," he said. "Something happens to you, it happens to me."

"Todo bien," Matt said again.

FIFTEEN

Their next practice was Monday night, before the Glenallen game.

Matt still hadn't talked to Ben about swinging at that 3-0 pitch. He didn't know if Sarge had talked to Ben about it, either. Now Matt wondered if Sarge would handle it at practice, or not at all.

But before they took the field, Sarge said he wanted to talk to the whole team. It wasn't about signs, as it turned out, wasn't about when to swing and when to take. It was about baseball. It was about being on a team.

"This isn't basketball," Sarge said. "In basketball, I swear, I've always thought that LeBron could walk into a gym or onto a playground court and find four guys and make them good enough to get into the playoffs. It's different in our game. It just is. An awful lot of people will tell you Mike Trout is the best all-around player. But he's already proven, as great as he is, that he can't take the Angels to the playoffs all by himself."

Sarge was seated on the pitcher's rubber. The Astros were in a small circle in front of him, on the grass between the mound and home plate.

"In baseball," he continued, "it's all about figuring out what's best for you and what's best for the team. Sometimes those two things are the same. But sometimes they're not. That's where I come in. Sometimes I have to tell you that what you want to do, and what you think is *best* for you, might not be best for our team. So I have to say something. Because what I want and what's best for me is *always* best for the South Shore Astros." He grinned. "That's why they put Sarge in charge."

They groaned.

"Couldn't help myself," Sarge said.

Then he nodded at Matt and his teammates.

"You guys understand what I'm talking about here?" Sarge said.

Matt, who was closest to Sarge, turned around and saw his teammates nodding.

"Good," he said. "We've only played one game, and none of us liked the way it came out. But we've got a chance to clear all that up tomorrow. But the thing I want to leave you all with is that you're not just playing for yourselves, you're not playing for your parents, you're not playing to please me. You're playing for each other. And if I see that you're not, and you don't understand that, I will sit your butt down. As much as that won't please me."

He stood up.

"Now let's play some baseball," he said. "Too nice a night not to."

Matt had gotten Sarge's message, loud and clear. He wondered if Ben had. He wondered if Ben understood that even though Sarge had been talking to the whole team, he'd really only been talking to Ben.

It was cool, Matt thought.

He'd found a way to call Ben out without calling him out.

Sarge in charge.

Matt knew Ben had been listening.

Now he hoped Ben had really heard.

· · ·

It was a good practice. Ben hit one of his monster home runs, but actually managed to hit a couple of solid lines, too. It seemed to surprise him as much as it surprised the rest of them.

He didn't seem to have shortened his swing. It didn't look as if he'd really changed anything. Maybe he was just able to concentrate on using a more level swing tonight, at least a few times, rather than his usual big uppercut.

But Ben had been born with that uppercut.

When he did manage to level it off, though, he didn't just hit line drives. He hit screamers. Matt hoped he could hit some like that tomorrow night against the Glenallen Giants, just in case there came a moment in the game when his team didn't need a monster home run.

Just a clean knock.

"How'd you like those swings?" Ben said after they'd all finished batting practice.

"I like watching all your swings," Matt said. Then he grinned and said, "I just like some better than others."

Ben's face was serious.

"I know," he said.

It was as if his face was telling Matt more than his words were.

"Hey," Matt said. "It's early."

He wasn't trying to make Ben feel better. It *was* early. They'd only played one game. But one of Sarge's absolute favorite baseball expressions came from the old Yankee catcher, Yogi Berra, whom Matt knew had played on ten Yankee World Series teams in his career.

"It sure gets late early around here," Yogi Berra had said once.

It looked funny when you read it. But Yogi was making sense. If the Astros lost their second game of the season, to the Glenallen Giants, if their record fell to 0–2, they were the ones who'd start to feel as if things were getting late in All-Stars, even after just one week.

"I guess I'll have to figure things out on my own," Ben said.

"I'm here if you need me," Matt said.

Ben gave him a funny look.

"I don't need anybody in the other sports," he said. "Not even my dad."

Matt didn't say anything. It wasn't because he couldn't get the words out. It was because he didn't know exactly what to say in the moment.

"No big secret that Sarge was talking about me before practice today," he said.

"I thought he was talking to all of us," Matt said.

"No," Ben said. "He was talking about me taking a hero swing on that three-oh pitch."

"Y-y-."

Matt swallowed, then took a big gulp of air. He could feel the words coming.

For now, he imagined himself checking a swing.

"Y-you have to pick your spots," he finally managed. "Y-you can't swing for the fences every single time."

"Maybe it's how who I am, and it'll be too hard to change," Ben said.

"Hitting is hard for everybody," Matt said. "Everybody says that hitting a pitched ball is the hardest thing to do in sports."

"My dad thinks I can grow up to be Judge or Stanton," Ben said.

Matt couldn't let that one go. It was too good a pitch to hit.

"Does he know how much Aaron Judge walks?" Matt said. "He walked a hundred and twenty-seven times the year he finished second in the MVP voting. And you know how many hits he had that year? One hundred fifty-four."

"He still hit fifty-one homers," Ben said.

"Yeah," Matt said. "And got more than a hundred hits that weren't home runs."

Matt felt as if he was standing on firm ground again, no hesitation, speaking fluent baseball.

"All my dad cares about is the home runs," Ben said.

"But Judge got great because he became a more disciplined

hitter," Matt said. "It's not just me saying that. Everybody does. There were times the Yankees even talked about making him a leadoff hitter."

"I'm the opposite of disciplined," Ben said, then shrugged. "I just want to have fun."

"All I'm telling you is that it doesn't have to be all or nothing and you can still have fun," Matt said. "Home runs or strike-outs. I get that Judge strikes out a lot too. But he wouldn't be the player he is if he didn't get on base as much as he does, and put the ball in play as much as he does."

"I'm never going to take baseball as seriously as you," Ben said.

At least they agreed on something.

SIXTEEN

Matt and his mom were eating one of his mom's specialties at their late dinner, homemade lasagna, with a salad on the side.

As they ate, he finally got around to telling her what had happened at the ice cream truck the day before. She listened in silence, letting Matt tell it his way, not changing expression. He could have been talking about baseball practice. Matt made it through the whole story, everything he'd said, everything he'd tried to say, the girls behind him, all of it. Including how he saw it all coming and felt it all coming as soon as he saw the line.

When Matt was finished, his mom reached across the table and put her hand over his, and squeezed.

"You got through it," she said. "That's the important thing."

"Barely," he said.

"I don't care how," she said. "I just know that you didn't get out of that line."

"Thought about it," Matt said.

Now his mom smiled.

"I know that sometimes there's things you can't say when you want to," she said. "But what's more important to your dad and me is the things you can. And the things you simply won't give in on."

Matt put down his fork.

"I don't want every single day of the rest of my life to be like this," he said.

"They won't be," she said.

"Feels like," Matt said.

"Sometimes," she said. "Just not all the time."

"You know another reason I felt bad yesterday?" Matt said to his mom. "Because José felt bad. It was like my problem had become his."

"Sounds to me as if José handled things just about perfectly," she said.

"He's cool."

"So," his mom said, "are you."

He had cleaned his plate of lasagna by then. His mom told him there was more. Matt said he was full. She raised an eyebrow. "Too full for strawberry shortcake?" she said.

"Are you kidding?" he said to his mom. "I didn't even get my strawberry ice cream yesterday!"

She laughed. So did he. It was funny, he thought, sometimes he didn't want to talk. Or couldn't talk. But sometimes when he was with his mom like this, he couldn't stop.

"Can't lie, Mom," he said. "When stuff like what happened at the truck happens, it makes me feel smaller than I already am. And weak."

She smiled again.

"You know who I'm looking at right now?" she said. "The toughest kid I know."

He started to say something. She put up a finger to stop him.

"I don't just see a tough kid who happens to be my kid," she said. "I see somebody who got to the front of that line and found a way to be bigger than the moment."

"How come I can do all the things I want to do in baseball," he said, "and sometimes I can't even order a stupid ice cream cone?"

"Hey," she said, pointing a finger at him now. "Ice cream is *never* stupid!"

"Mom," he said, "I'm trying to be serious."

"Ice cream *is* serious," she said.

"I want to be like everybody else," Matt said.

"No chance," she said. "You're never going to be like everybody else, in all the best possible ways. You're you, honey. You're fast and strong and sweet. You've been fearless your whole life, no matter how many times you were the smallest boy in the game. And you stutter. You've overcome your size and you'll overcome that, as much as anybody can. That's it. The whole package. Like you're the whole package."

"Thanks," Matt said.

"No thanks required," she said. "Just keeping it real, dog."

Matt shook his head.

"Maybe that was a thought that should have stayed inside *your* head," he said.

"I'm so ashamed," she said, putting her head down, and then the two of them were laughing again.

"You're the one who's the whole package, Mom," Matt said.

"No kidding!" she said.

They cleaned up the dishes. His mom washed them by hand. Matt dried. Then they both had strawberry shortcake with fresh-whipped cream. As usual, Matt finished all of his and then half of his mom's when she offered it to him. She said she shouldn't have had any dessert, she was in training.

"For what?" Matt said.

"For starters," she said, "keeping up with you. Because that always feels as if it ought to be an Olympic event."

"That's funny," he said to her. "I always feel as if it's the other way around."

Before he went upstairs to watch baseball, his mom said, "How's Ben doing, by the way?"

Matt said, "Sometimes I can't decide whether it's his dad in his way, or he can't get out of his own way."

"Funny thing about this world of ours," his mom said. "Seems like everybody's got things that get in their way, doesn't it?"

When Matt was nearly out of the kitchen, his mom said, "Hey, I've got a question."

He turned.

"Shoot," he said.

"What did we have for dessert tonight?"

"Strawberry shortcake," he said.

This time "strawberry" came out of him as smoothly as dessert had gone down.

She winked at him.

"Piece of cake," she said.

SEVENTEEN

The game against the Giants was in Glenallen, which was just ten minutes north of South Shore, on a cool field that was so close to downtown it was as if somebody had built a Little League field in the town's backyard.

There were signs for local stores painted all along the outfield fence. There were no bleachers on the sides of the field, but there was a hill behind the outfield fence where people spread out blankets and set up lawn chairs and watched the game from there.

The Astros players knew that the Giants had won their first game, against the Putnam Pirates. So even though this was just the second game of the season, it felt like a big game. They didn't want to fall into an 0–2 hole, and already be two games behind the Giants or anybody else in the league.

"Sarge is right," Matt said to José and Denzel while they were seated on their bench waiting for the top of the first. "We get our chance to clean up the way our first game ended."

"Like cleaning our room!" Denzel said.

"I hate cleaning my room," José said.

Matt grinned. "Well," he said, "I hate being oh-and-one."

They all knew the Giants starting pitcher from last year's All-Stars. His name was Darryl Joseph, and the Astros players on the town basketball team knew him from hoops as well. Kyle Sargent, a star guard for the South Shore team, said that not only did Darryl look like Kevin Durant, he could shoot like a madman from the outside.

But he could really pitch, too. His delivery, just as Matt remembered from last season, was straight over the top. And as tall as Darryl was, his fastball seemed to explode on you out of the sky. Even now they could hear the pop in the catcher's glove as he took his last warm-up pitches. For a pitcher, that sound was like the one you heard when a hitter caught a pitch on the sweet spot of his bat.

Mike Clark was pitching for the Astros. José was leading off again. Teddy Sample, playing left tonight, was batting second for their second game. Matt was behind Teddy. Stone Russell had moved up to cleanup and Ben was hitting behind him. It wasn't a big surprise that Sarge had juggled the batting order a little. He'd told them at their first practice that he'd be doing that.

"You get to do everything on this team except get too comfortable," was the way their coach had explained it.

It was fine with Matt. As proud as he was to be in the three hole, he didn't care where he was in Sarge's order, as long as he was in there somewhere.

Matt took a quick look to the hill in the outfield, and saw his mom sitting with Denzel's mom on a blanket. José's parents were next to them.

"It looks like they're ready to have a picnic out there," Ben said.

"Is your dad here tonight?" Matt asked him.

"Nah, he had to go out of town on business. He'll be back for our game against the Pirates on Saturday. All good."

Really good, Matt thought.

"Facing Darryl is going to be no picnic," Denzel said.

"No worries," José said. "We're going to eat this guy's lunch."

He was standing now, bat in his hands, ready to lead off the game.

Sarge had come up behind them.

"You guys are starting to make me hungry," he said.

"Hungry for a win," Matt said.

Sarge leaned in and said, "Let's jump on that big kid with the ball early."

He jogged over to the third-base coaching box. Teddy Sample's dad was coaching first tonight. José was ready to hit. Teddy was in the on-deck circle. Stone sat next to Matt. Ben was on the other side of Stone. And Matt got the same rush of excitement he felt before every game he played, excitement and nerves. But he knew they were good nerves in this cool ballpark, in a town not far from his own.

He could hear Ben and Stone talking next to him, but couldn't really hear a word they were saying, because he was focused on watching Darryl Joseph pitch to José, who took his first fastball for a strike. The pop in the catcher's glove sounded even louder than it had during warm-ups. Game on.

José wasn't up there long, striking out on three pitches. But then Darryl walked Teddy and it was Matt's turn to step into the batter's box.

Now it was him against Darryl.

"Jump on him early," Sarge had said.

The Giants catcher said, "Hey, you're the little dude."

He said it after Matt had given a quick tap to the catcher's shin guards, the way he always did his first time at bat, the way guys did in the big leagues. It was part greeting, part respect.

Matt didn't say anything back. He didn't know their catcher. He'd heard variations of "little dude" and "little guy" plenty of times before. By now he heard it and he didn't. It was just part of the noise of the game.

So he didn't look down at the catcher, or acknowledge that he *had* heard. He just went through his routine, pulling on the brim of his batting helmet, checking his stance, now tapping the plate with the end of his bat.

Then he stepped out, because Darryl Joseph had stepped off the rubber to tie one of his shoes.

The catcher wasn't done chirping.

"Hey," he said to Matt, "can you see over the plate?"

Matt wasn't going to respond to that, either. But the home plate umpire did.

"I want you to stop talking to the batter now, son," the ump said.

Darryl stood up. Matt stepped back into the box. He was ready to hit.

More than ready.

MIKE LUPICA

"I was just kidding around," the catcher said.

"Well, I'm not, son," the ump said. "I don't want to hear you trash-talking anybody for the rest of this game."

He didn't say it loudly. He really only said it loud enough for the catcher and Matt to hear. But the catcher shut up then. Matt stared out at Darryl Joseph.

Be ready.

Be Altuve, he told himself.

They always said that he came out of the dugout swinging.

Darryl had a high leg kick, and what the announcers on television would call a windmill motion, a lot of arms and legs before the ball came out of his hand, and out of the sky.

It was a fastball.

Matt jumped on it, just like Sarge had said, and knew he'd gotten all of it. This was *his* sound. It was a shot to right-center, splitting the center fielder and the right fielder.

Matt was running hard out of the box, able to track the ball with his eyes, cutting the bag at first the way he'd been taught and flying toward second. As he got to second, he could see Sarge behind third base. Now Sarge was the one windmilling his right arm, telling him to go for three.

Fine with me.

Teddy was already across the plate with their team's first run. Sarge put his hands up, telling Matt he didn't need to slide.

Then suddenly he was waving his right arm like a madman again. Matt came around third and gave a quick look over his shoulder, and saw the ball rolling away from the Giants second baseman, who must have been the cut-off man for the throw from the outfield.

Matt got back up to full speed as quickly as he could.

Heading home.

Teddy was standing next to the plate, telling him to slide. Matt did. If he accidentally sprayed a little extra dirt on the catcher, well, those were just the breaks of the game.

Even if it wasn't a real inside-the-park home run, even if there had been some kind of error on the play, either on the cut-off throw or the catch, Matt didn't care, not even a little bit.

It *felt* like one. Felt like he'd cleared the fence and hit one all the way up on the hill where his mom and the other parents were sitting on their blankets and chairs.

It was 2–0, Astros.

Matt popped right up, clapping his hands. The throw from the second baseman had bounced in front of him, and then behind him. The catcher hadn't chased it. Instead, he was standing on the plate, way too close to Matt.

They didn't come into contact. But they nearly did.

"Hey," the catcher said to Matt, "you bumped me."

Now the ump took off his mask. Matt could see that he was smiling.

"First of all, son, he didn't, because I was standing right here," the ump said. "And second, what part of me telling you to stop talking to the other team didn't you understand?"

The Glenallen coach came over then. *He* told the catcher to stop talking and just play the game. Matt didn't say a word, just took a high five from Teddy as the two of them turned around and walked back to their bench. Stone struck out then. Ben gave the first pitch *he* saw from Darryl a ride, but the center fielder tracked it down a few feet from the fence.

As the Astros took the field for the bottom of the first, Ben asked Matt what the catcher had said to him, both times.

Matt told him.

"Guy's a jerk," Ben said.

Matt grinned, then motioned for Ben to lean down so only he could hear.

"I've met bigger," he said.

Darryl Joseph settled down over the next few innings. Mike Clark gave up an unearned run in the second, after a two-out error by Kyle Sargent at third. The Giants first baseman hit a home run in the fourth to tie the game at two all.

The Astros left the bases loaded in the top of the third.

José singled and, after Teddy struck out, Darryl walked Matt. Then, amazingly, Ben took a walk, twice laying off high fastballs he usually couldn't resist. It made Matt think that maybe Ben's dad should skip more games. But Stone struck out, and so did Kyle Sargent, and the game stayed tied.

Mike was out of the game by the fifth inning. Sarge brought in the Astros closer, Pat McQuade, knowing that Pat could easily pitch two innings if he needed to.

The Giants catcher hadn't said another word to Matt. Even though the kid—by now Matt knew his first name was Joey—had as big a mouth as he did, he had to know, *being* a catcher, that it wouldn't help him or his team to annoy the home plate umpire any more than he had in the first inning.

When Matt got to the plate in the top of the fifth, there were two outs and nobody on. It didn't change Matt's focus, or his approach. He hated to make the last out of an inning almost as much as he hated making the last out of a game.

Just get on base somehow, he told himself.

He took no notice of the catcher as he took his stance, went through his routine, took a borderline pitch for strike one. Then he laid off two pitches in the dirt.

It was 2-1.

Hitter's count.

The Giants relief pitcher wasn't a big guy. But he could

throw pretty hard, and Matt saw how much natural sink his fastball had as the kid was getting ground ball outs from José and Teddy.

He tried to come inside with the 2-1 pitch. But the ball got away from him, and ended up too far inside. Matt tried to get out of the way, couldn't do that in time, and the ball clipped him on his left elbow. It didn't really hurt. But it got him.

"Take your base," the ump said right away.

Matt turned and handed his bat to Stone, who was walking toward the plate from the on-deck circle. He was starting to jog down to first base when he heard the catcher say, "He faked it."

Matt stopped, and turned.

"The ball hit him," the ump said.

"No, it didn't," the catcher said. "Why don't you ask him?"

"I don't have to ask him," the ump said. "Now I want everybody to do what I told them to do at the start of the game: Play ball."

But Joey, the catcher, wouldn't stop talking. Matt stood there watching, and wondered if he might be talking himself right out of the game.

"Okay," Joey said, still in his crouch, but looking right at Matt now. "I'll ask: Did that ball really hit you?"

Matt didn't just feel the catcher's eyes on him. He felt the eyes of everybody on the field.

It was as if he were back in the ice cream line at Healey Park.

"Y-y-y . . ."

There was no place to go. No place to run, not even to first base.

All he had to say was "Yes."

Matt could feel himself wanting to explode. He tried to breathe through his nose, as a way of relaxing himself. He could feel himself clenching his fists, the way his jaw was clenched.

"Just take your base," the ump said to Matt. To the catcher he said, "One more word and you can take the rest of the game off."

Then Matt heard Ben say, "I've got one more word."

The Astros' bench was on the first-base side of the field. Ben had walked out and was standing between Matt and Joey.

"Yes," Ben said.

"Didn't ask you," Joey said.

He was standing by now, but seemed to take a step back from Ben, almost without realizing he had.

"But I'm answering you," Ben said. "You talk to one of us, you talk to all of us."

The ump said to Ben, "You head back to the bench, son."

He told the catcher to get ready to catch. He looked at

Matt and just pointed at first base. Ben was still standing next to Matt.

Now Matt was able to speak.

"Thank you," he said.

Ben leaned down and said, "Guess sometimes it's okay for me to finish sentences for you."

He was smiling as he said it. Matt didn't think he was kidding. He went to first. Ben went to get his bat, then headed for the on-deck circle, ready to hit if Stone Russell kept the inning going.

They were back to baseball now, game still tied, waiting for somebody to win it.

Matt was running on anything. So he was running hard from first when Stone lined a ball over the second baseman's head and into right field. Sarge waved him to third. There was no throw. Matt went in standing up.

First and third.

Ben at the plate.

He took a huge cut, and missed, for strike one.

He did the same thing for strike two, the second swing looking even wilder than the first.

Ben had put himself in the hole, that quickly, by once again trying to swing right out of his shoes.

Ben being Ben, Matt thought, whether his dad was urging

him on or not. So maybe it wasn't as much Ben's dad as he said. Maybe he was the hitter he wanted to be. Maybe he didn't really want to change, even though he'd said he did.

Matt knew what had to happen next. The Giants pitcher had to throw the next pitch—or two—anywhere except the strike zone. He had to be careful about throwing one in the dirt, because if it got past the catcher and got to the screen, Matt was coming home.

But he couldn't throw Ben anything good. All he needed to do was allow Big Ben to get himself out, which is what Matt was sure was about to happen.

Only the pitcher didn't waste a pitch, or try to make Ben chase.

He threw him a strike.

And Ben didn't miss.

He hit one high and deep to left field. The only question once it was in the air was if it would stay fair. It did. When it came down, it came down *over* the fans sitting on their blankets and chairs, and nearly made it to the street behind them.

To Ben's credit, he didn't pose in the batter's box. He ran hard out of the box even though he had to know better than anyone that the ball was gone the moment he hit it. Only when the ball came down did he slow down.

It was 5–2 for the Astros.

Matt and Stone waited for Ben at home plate. Matt worried, briefly, that he might say something to Joey. But he didn't.

He said something to Matt before they got back to their bench:

"Was that swing too long?"

EIGHTEEN

"Why do you think Ben even asked you for help in the first place?" José said.

They had gone for ice cream at the Candy Kitchen when they'd gotten back from Glenallen. Matt had managed to make his order without any problems this time. Two scoops of strawberry.

Refusing to take the easy way out.

Making the same order he couldn't the other day.

Now he and José were sitting on a bench in front of the Candy Kitchen, going back over the game with the Giants, pretty much from start to finish. They talked about what Joey, the Giants catcher, had said to Matt. They talked about Ben walking over from the bench to say something to Joey when Matt couldn't, and about what Ben had said about finishing Matt's sentences.

Finally they talked about what Ben had said about his home run swing when the game was over, sarcastically asking Matt if it had been too long.

"Weird, right?" Matt said to José. "He should have been totally happy about winning the game and it was almost as if he was mad at me."

"He's usually not like that," José said.

"He was like that today," Matt said.

"It *is* weird," José said, "because he does seem to care what you think."

"Here's what *I* think," Matt said. "I just tried to help him. And you're right, it's not like I went to him and asked to be his batting coach."

"Maybe it's like you said, and he never really wanted to change, but he wanted you to think that he did," José said. "Does that make sense?"

"Why would he care so much about what I think?" Matt said. "I'm just another guy on our team."

"If you really think that," José said, grinning, "then let me give you a real easy Spanish word you can use: You're *loco*."

They heard somebody calling their names then, and looked up and saw Kyle waving at them from his dad's car as they went through town. Matt and José waved back. It was good to be an Astro today. They had played well and won a game. They had gotten on the board. Sarge always talked about how important it was to score the first run of a game. It felt more important today to have their first win.

"It didn't bother me as much what he said about his swing than what he said about finishing my sentences," Matt said.

"Maybe he just took it the wrong way when you asked him not to do that," José said. "But it wasn't like you were singling him out. We all know the deal. You want to work your way through stuff yourself."

"What I really don't get," Matt said, "is why he even came out to talk to their catcher in the first place."

Matt felt his phone buzzing then. He took it out of his pocket and saw that it was his mom, telling him she'd be there to pick them up in about ten minutes.

"You know what I think?" José said. "I think that maybe Ben is more complicated than he looks sometimes."

"I'm not looking to be his best friend," Matt said. "Sometimes you don't get to decide who your friends are. But I want to be the best friend to him that I can be, and the best teammate."

"So just keep doing what you're doing," José said. "Because what we found out today is how important both of you are to our team."

"It's not just Ben and me," Matt said. "We can't win without you playing your best, either. And if you don't think that, you're the one who's *loco*."

José smiled.

"You're Altuve," he said. "He's Judge."

"And who's your favorite shortstop?" Matt said.

"You know it's Carlos Correa," José said. "He plays next to Altuve for the Astros the way I play next to you."

"Then you're Correa on our Astros," Matt said.

They bumped fists.

"Thanks for the compliment!" José said.

In a quiet voice Matt said, "Thanks for being such a good friend."

NINETEEN

Matt had an appointment with Ms. Francis, the day before the Astros' next practice and two days before their game against the Putnam Mets.

"So what's new?" Ms. Francis said when Matt sat down.

"A lot," Matt said.

He told her everything that had happened since their last visit. He told her about freezing up when the Glenallen catcher asked him if he'd really gotten hit by that pitch. He told her the things Ben said.

Matt didn't rush. He didn't stop. He didn't *want* to stop. The words came spilling out of him today. There were times when he could talk like this with his mom. His mom was just about the smartest person he knew. But Ms. Francis was smart too. Sometimes he wanted to be in this room with her, and not outside.

"Of the things you just described," she said, "what bothered you the most?"

Matt didn't answer right away. Ms. Francis liked to say that serious questions required serious answers.

"Ben," he said.

"Did you think he was being mean by asking if it was all right to complete a sentence?" she said.

That was a question Matt kept asking himself.

"I don't *think* he's mean," Matt said finally. "I've never seen Ben go out of his way to be mean to somebody else. And I can't get too mad at him, because he was out there speaking up for me when their catcher called me out the way he did."

He stopped.

"What is it?" Ms. Francis said.

It was as if in that moment Matt had chosen silence, instead of silence choosing him the way it did sometimes.

"I was just thinking how ashamed I was when I couldn't speak for myself to that guy."

"The catcher," she said.

"Yes," Matt said.

"We've talked about that," she said. "You know there's nothing to feel ashamed *about*."

"I can tell myself that all I want," Matt said. "You can tell me that all *you* want. And my mom can. But those feelings don't go away. That doesn't change."

"But you're changing," she said. "Whether you realize you are or not. I can hear it during our sessions. You understand yourself a lot better than you did before we first began meeting."

"But the other day, when I just stood there feeling like a dummy all over again," Matt said. "I felt worse than when I got to the front of the ice cream line."

A robin landed on the windowsill behind Ms. Francis, stared in at them, then flew away, as if it didn't have a care in the world.

"Why was it worse?" Ms. Francis said.

"Because it was baseball," Matt said.

He could feel himself stepping hard on "baseball," the way you stepped hard on home plate sometimes.

"Baseball is supposed to be your safe place," she said in a gentle voice.

"Yes," Matt said.

"Yes." The word he couldn't get out of his mouth for the Glenallen catcher.

"It was like everything at once," Matt said. "It was that scared feeling that comes over me when I get called on in class and I'm not ready with an answer. I don't just feel like everyone in class is looking at me, and waiting for me. I feel as if the whole world is waiting for me to say something I can't."

"Has it ever happened to you before?" she said. "On a ball field, I mean."

"Not like that," he said. "I mean, I know it started because that kid was acting like a jerk. But I felt that my mom and the parents sitting in the outfield were staring at me too, even though I knew they couldn't hear what was going on."

"Then when it was over, it wasn't the catcher you thought was making fun of you," she said.

Matt shook his head.

"I don't think the catcher was making fun of me," Matt said. "I don't think he knew I stutter. I think he was just messing with me, the way he had been when he asked if I could see over the plate."

"What he said about you being small didn't bother you?" Ms. Francis said.

"Not saying I like it," Matt said. "But I'm used to it by now."

"But then Ben was the one messing with you," she said, "even after standing up for you."

"Yeah," he said.

"And how did that make you feel?" she said.

"Small," Matt said.

Now they were both silent.

"Maybe," Ms. Francis said finally, "you don't know Ben as well as you thought you did."

"And he doesn't know me," Matt said.

"Maybe," Ms. Francis said, "you and Ben need to talk things out one of these days."

Matt smiled.

"Oh, great," he said. "More talking."

Just what he needed.

TWENTY

Matt's mom asked if he minded if she watched his whole practice tonight. He said he'd love it.

"I know some of the other dads come and hang out from the time practice starts," she said. "Why should they get to have all the fun?"

Matt grinned. "Is there a good answer for that other than 'no?'" he said.

"No!" she said.

"You know as much about baseball as most of those dads, and probably more," Matt said. "You know as much as Sarge."

"Let's keep that last part between the two of us," she said.

Then she sounded like a little kid when she asked, "Do you think I should bring my glove?"

"Absolutely," Matt said.

She had her glove on her left hand when she and Matt came walking onto the field at Healey Park. As soon as Sarge saw that, he said, "You know I'm going to put you to work, right?"

"Send me in, coach," she said.

"Would you rather work with the infielders or the outfielders?"

"Well," she said, "having been to both games your team has played so far, I do think your second baseman needs a little work on fundamentals."

"You know," Sarge said, "I was thinking the same thing."

"The two of you are *so* funny," Matt said.

"You work with Matt and Ben and José and Kyle," Sarge said to her. "I'll be in the outfield."

"Deal," Rachel Baker said.

She went over to where Matt had dropped his bat bag and took out his bat. Then she walked over to home plate, where Stone was waiting for her. The rest of the infielders took their positions.

Before they started, José put his glove in front of his mouth and said to Matt, "Your mom, dude. Really?"

"Just watch," Matt said.

There was no reason why any of them should have known how much game she'd had when she was young. But Matt knew. He knew that his baseball mom could do all the things that baseball dads could do. She had pitched in softball and played shortstop when she wasn't pitching. And Matt knew, from reading up on her, that she could *really* swing a bat back in the day.

He also knew from the times when it had been just the two of them on this same field, and they'd brought one of her old softballs with her, and Matt had pitched to her and seen her spray line drives all over the place. One day he had said to her, "You know, your swing looks a lot like mine."

"Other way around, buster," she'd said.

At the plate now she called out to the Astros infielders and said, "You boys ready to work?"

She didn't wait for an answer, and immediately smacked a hard ground ball at Kyle Sargent, who fielded it cleanly and threw a strike across the infield grass to Ben.

After that they *did* work, and hard. She hit hard ground balls at all of them, and to their left, and right. Every once in a while, she'd mix in a slow roller, to make sure they were paying attention. Then she started to call out game situations, telling them to throw home as if there were a play at the plate, or telling Ben to start a 1-6-3 double play, or simply yelling out, "Turn two!" before she'd hit a rocket right at Matt.

She was smiling the whole time, and looked completely happy.

After they'd successfully turned a few double plays, she suddenly choked up on the bat and laid down a perfect bunt in front of Ben, the ball dying between home and first before he could get to it.

"I wasn't expecting a bunt, Mrs. Baker," Ben said after he finally picked up the ball.

"The other team isn't going to make an announcement either," she said.

A few minutes later, she tried to surprise Ben with another bunt. He was ready this time. He closed quickly on the ball, barehanded it, did a neat spin, and made a perfect throw to Matt, who had sprinted over to cover first.

Matt thought to himself, *Maybe my mom should have tried to be Ben's batting coach.*

But right now, she was coaching up everybody, but good. Even Matt. One time he made what he thought was a really sweet backhand stop near second base, stopped himself, and snapped off a sure throw to Ben.

But his mom said, "You should never have had to backhand that ball, Matt Baker. You had enough time to get in front of it."

"Are you gonna ground him, Mrs. Baker?" José called in to her.

"No," she said. "But if it happens again, no dessert."

"I made the play, Mom," Matt said.

"Yes," she said. "It just wasn't the right play. Isn't *that* right?"

The answer came right out of him.

"Yes, Mom," he said.

Sarge had finished with the outfielders a few minutes ago, and had been watching from the bench as Matt's mom put him and the guys through their infield drills. When they finished, and had come over for a water break, Sarge said to Rachel Baker, "What would you think about becoming my permanent first base coach?"

"Are you serious?" she said. "I haven't even made it through a whole practice yet."

"Totally serious," he said. "You run a better practice than I do."

"Not sure about that," she said. "But before I give you my answer, let me get one out of my friend at second base."

She turned to Matt and said, "What do you think?"

"I think," Matt said, "that I need to start calling you Coach Mom."

Then his mom turned back to Sarge, cool as could be, and bumped him some fist as if she were an Astro already.

"I'm in," she said.

As José and Matt were grabbing their water bottles, José leaned in close to Matt and said, "What just happened here?"

"Pretty sure my mom just became one of the boys," he said.

When it was time for the Astros to take batting practice, Matt walked over to his mom and said, "You know you're not getting to hit, right?"

She lightly slapped the side of her head with her hand in mock anger and said, "Darn it! I was afraid of that."

The only thing that changed from one batting practice to another was the order. Tonight Ben got to lead off. His swing looked the same as it always did. He didn't try to hit to the opposite field. Didn't try to use all fields. Just tried to go deep. He finally did on his second-to-last swing. He didn't seem to be trying to go to right field, but did. If the clump of trees behind the right field fence hadn't gotten in the way, Matt imagined the ball rolling all the way to the South Shore train station.

"Well, that swing definitely wasn't too long," Matt said.

Ben looked at him, as if confused. Maybe he didn't even remember what he'd said to Matt the other night.

"Huh?"

"Just saying that was some shot," Matt said, and put up his hand for a high five as a way of ending the conversation. Sometimes it was better not to say anything.

BP was the last thing they did that night. By the time they finished, a lot of the other parents had already arrived for pickup, including Ben's dad.

Matt and his mom were standing near the screen behind home plate.

"So how was my first night as a coach?" she said to Matt.

Before he could answer, Ben said, "For a mom, you did awesome, Mrs. Baker."

Matt didn't think Ben was trying to be funny, or sarcastic. It was, Matt thought, his way of being nice. He was smiling. So was she. But then they heard Sarge whistle, and say, "Uh oh? *For a mom?*"

Matt saw Ben's face redden.

"I was just trying to give Mrs. Baker a compliment," he said.

"And I thank you for that, Ben," she said. "But Matt can tell you: In our house, we sort of don't think there was ever a law passed that only dads know baseball."

"Do you know what a great softball player Matt's mom was?" Sarge said.

Ben said, "I think Matt might have told us."

"Well, back in the day," Sarge said, winking at Matt's mom, "she was the best pitcher in the state. And probably the best player."

He went over to the ball bag then and reached around inside

and came out with a softball that looked older than Healey Park.

Then he looked around at the Astros players and said, "Who wants to take a few cuts against her right now?"

Matt wasn't putting up his hand. There had been times when he'd asked her to show him her fastball. Mostly what he'd done, even against the bigger ball, was swing and miss. A lot. No way he was going to let her make him look bad in front of his teammates. And he knew his mom well enough to know that she wasn't going to want to look bad in front of the team.

No one spoke until Ben's dad called out, "You do it, Ben."

Ben didn't look over at him. He looked at Matt's mom. As if Matt's mom could somehow save him from his own dad.

"I don't want to hit against you, Mrs. Baker," he said.

"And you don't have to if you don't want to," she said in a quiet voice.

"C'mon, Ben," his dad said. "Let's see how far you can hit one of those balls."

"Maybe this isn't such a good idea," Rachel Baker said to Sarge.

But he was smiling.

"Be a good way to for these boys to see how good the girls are in this sport," he said.

"What if I hit one right back up the middle?" Ben said, even though Matt knew Ben hardly ever went right back up the middle.

"I'm still pretty good with a glove," Matt's mom said, "even for an old lady."

The Astros players were into this now. Stone put his chest protector and mask back on. Matt asked Sarge if he wanted the rest of the Astros to go back into the field. But Mr. Roberson heard that and laughed and said, "Not gonna need any fielders, Matt."

Matt's mom put her glove back on, took the ball from Sarge, headed out to the mound, where she soft-tossed a few warm-up pitches, picking up steam on the last few.

"Wait," Ben said, "you're going to pitch *underhand*?"

"Big Ben," Sarge said, "have you ever watched a softball game?"

"Not exactly," Ben said.

"They throw pretty hard underhand," Matt said to Ben.

"Guess I'm about to find out how hard," Ben said.

Matt wasn't sure his mom threw her first pitch as hard as she could. But she threw it hard enough. Ben didn't seem to be ready for it at all, but managed to get his bat on the ball and hit a weak grounder up the first base line.

Ben stepped out. Matt could see how determined he was to

do better on the next pitch. He didn't want to look bad.

Matt didn't think his mom wanted Ben to look bad, either. But she was clearly having fun with this.

"Here comes my heater," she said.

It was funny, Matt thought, watching from behind the screen. If there were ever a time for Ben Roberson *to* shorten his swing, now was that time.

The second pitch came in hotter, and higher, than the first. Ben took his usual big cut, and missed.

Strike two.

"Just relax, big man," Ben's dad yelled over from behind the Astros' bench. "This is your pitch."

Matt's mom didn't throw the third pitch as high, or as hard. Matt was pretty sure that she would have been perfectly happy for Ben to put a charge into one.

Matt could see how tightly Ben was gripping the handle of the bat, holding it all the way down to the knob the way he always did.

He found himself rooting for Ben against his mom, just wanting him to put the ball in play somewhere.

The pitch came right down the middle, but Ben was trying way too hard to hit a home run, and swung over the pitch for strike three.

This time Ben was the one who seemed speechless. His dad

wasn't. He wasn't yelling out to Ben this time. He only seemed to be talking to himself, and turned away from the field.

But Matt could hear him clearly as he said, "Terrific. My kid just got struck out by a girl."

TWENTY-ONE

Matt turned back to the field and saw his mom go into her full mom mode, since now Ben Roberson had every-body on a baseball field staring at him.

"You struck out on purpose, didn't you, Ben Roberson?" she said, hands on her hips.

"No, Mrs. Baker," Ben said in a quiet voice.

She was smiling her biggest smile.

"I don't want your pity!" she said. "If we ever do this again, you have to promise to try to get a hit, okay?"

"Okay," he said.

Matt smiled to himself, watching her try to get everybody past this moment, and thought:

My mom might just have gotten her one and only save of the season.

She jogged in from the mound and bumped Ben some fist and said, "Thanks for making the old lady look good."

"No worries, Mrs. Baker," Ben said.

They walked off the field together. As they did, Matt heard her say to Ben, "Mind if I give you a quick batting tip? It might help you when you *are* trying to get a hit."

"Sure," Ben said.

"I'd listen to her," Sarge said. "She's always telling me Matt got his swing from her."

"Sure," Ben said again.

She didn't talk about shortening his swing. She didn't talk about leveling it off, or anything like that. She just grabbed his bat and went and took her stance.

"I noticed you've got a pretty big leg kick," she said, "when you're trying to drive the ball."

As if he wasn't always trying to drive the ball into outer space.

"I've always swung that way," Ben said.

"Well," she said, "I watch a lot of baseball on TV with Matt, and the other night they were talking about how high Shohei Ohtani's leg kick was when he first got over here from Japan. And how he struggled in his first spring training until he started tapping the toe of his front foot before he swung. It just seemed to quiet his swing at the time, and that's when he started driving the ball all over the place."

"Okay," Ben said.

"Just try it sometime and see if it might work for you," she said.

"I could try it now, even with the softball," Ben said, "if you don't mind hanging around."

"Ben!"

Mr. Roberson.

"We need to get going," he said, "if *softball* practice is over for now."

He looked at Matt's mom and said, "No offense, Rachel."

She smiled, but Matt knew she didn't mean it.

"None taken," she said. "My own son has to endure batting tips from me all the time."

"My son gets his batting tips from me, too," Mr. Roberson said.

Matt's mom handed Ben his bat back. He went and got his glove. He and his dad left. Matt and his mom and Sarge watched them go.

"I've got to wear this," Sarge said. "I shouldn't have let you pitch to him."

"His dad sort of insisted," Matt said.

"I hope I didn't offend Bob," Matt's mom said.

"He's a nice enough guy, in his own way," Sarge said. "But he's another dad who thinks he invented baseball."

"And his batting tips only seem to involve telling his son in a loud voice to crush one," she said.

Sarge sighed. "Tell me about it," he said.

"Are you absolutely certain you still want me to help you coach this team?" she said.

"More than ever, actually," Sarge said.

He grinned and turned to Matt and said, "Not going to be dull having your mom around."

"Never is," Matt said.

Nothing was dull these days, on or off the field.

TWENTY-TWO

Right before Matt was ready to turn out his lights and go to bed, his mom came into his room.

"We need to convene a family meeting," she said.

Matt felt himself smile.

"I don't think you have to take attendance," he said. "Everybody seems to be here."

"Well then, I guess we can start," she said.

"Sometimes," Matt said to her, "I forget which one of us acts more like a twelve-year-old."

"Got me there," she said.

"What's up?" he said.

"I don't have to do this," she said. "Be your assistant coach."

"You're not just my assistant coach, Mom," he said. "Pretty sure you'd be everybody's."

"But I'm not everybody's mom."

"Lucky for me," he said.

She smiled.

"Mom," he said, "you probably should have coached Little League way before this."

"It's different for a woman," she said. "And trust me, not just in baseball."

Matt sat up.

"I can tell how much you want to do this," he said. "We all saw how much fun you had tonight. Heck, you practically said yes to Sarge before he even finished asking you to do it."

"You're sure you want me to do this?"

"I want you to do this because I can see you want to do this," Matt said. "And just the guys in the infield know they all got a little better tonight, in about fifteen minutes."

"What about Ben?" she said.

Matt grinned.

"This is turning into a talk, isn't it?"

"Sometimes I can't help myself," she said.

"Ben will be fine," Matt said. "It's his dad I always worry about, Mom."

"Same," she said.

"He seems pretty set in his ways," Matt said.

"And maybe not just about baseball," his mom said. "When he said 'softball' tonight you know what he was really saying was 'girls' softball.'"

Matt didn't mention what he'd said about Ben being struck out by a girl.

"Seems to me," his mom continued, "that he's pretty stuck on how he thinks guys are supposed to act."

"Not sure I understand," Matt said.

"All the old stuff about how if guys don't act strong, that must mean they're weak, or soft," she said. She grinned. "That they're acting like girls."

She put air quotes around "girls."

"But you're the strongest person I know," Matt said to her.

She got up off the end of the bed and then leaned down and kissed him on top of his head.

"Thanks, pal," she said.

"You think that toe-tapping thing might make Ben a better hitter?" he said.

"Yup."

"Think he'll actually try it?"

"Hope so," she said.

She shrugged and said, "But only if his dad lets him."

"Think that will happen?" Matt said.

"Only if he thinks it's a guy thing," she said.

She didn't make "guy thing" sound like a good thing.

TWENTY-THREE

The next night Matt's mom was ready to go to Healey Park for the Astros' game against the Putnam Valley Mets before he was.

"Remember the other night when I had to remind you that you didn't get to take BP?" Matt said.

"It was hurtful," she said, "but yes."

"So you know you're just coaching and not playing tonight, correct?"

"You don't have to rub it in," she said.

She had her glove on the kitchen table. She was wearing an Astros cap that he'd never seen before. Matt asked if she'd bought the hat today.

"Might have remembered there's a Lids store at the mall," she said.

"Maybe think about curving the bill a little more," Matt said.

"Oh," she said, "you get to play *and* coach."

The game was scheduled for six-thirty. They were at the field an hour before that, before Sarge or any of the other Astros players, throwing on the side. When Sarge and the rest of Matt's teammates did show up and it was time for infield practice, Sarge said, "You handle it, Rachel. Guys on our team might as well start getting used to the idea that the two of us are a team, too."

Sarge worked with the outfielders, and then threw batting practice, the way he always did. As soon as it was Ben's turn, Matt noticed that Ben was lifting up his front foot the way he always did. He didn't hit any BP homers tonight, even if he came close on his last swing.

"*No worries, save it for the game!*"

Matt didn't even have to turn around to recognize Mr. Roberson's voice. He'd missed their last game, but obviously wasn't going to miss this one.

"*Let's get ready to play some old-fashioned hardball tonight!*"

Matt thought: *Everything about this family is big.*

Ben nodded to acknowledge that he'd heard his dad. But Matt was pretty sure they could hear him at the Candy Kitchen.

Matt was worried that it might be a long baseball night at Healey Park. Just not in a good way.

The Putnam Valley Mets were new to the All-Stars this year, so Matt and the guys didn't know any of their players.

"But they look good to me," José said.

"Everybody looks good to you," Denzel said.

"I like to be prepared," José said.

"You know what Sarge always says," Matt said. "They want to win too."

Then it was José quoting their coach.

"Expect them to do great things," he began.

". . . just the way we expect ourselves to do great things," Matt said.

"Wait a second!" José said. "You get to finish *my* sentences?"

Matt laughed. "*Lo siento mucho!*" he said.

So sorry.

Teddy Sample was starting tonight for the Astros, which meant Mike Clark was back in left field. Denzel was leading off, José was second, Matt was in his usual third spot.

Ben was back batting cleanup.

Matt looked up the Putnam Valley starter in Sarge's scorebook. His name was Tyler Brewer. Matt watched him warm up, the way he always watched the other team's starter warm up, after Teddy breezed through the top of the first, striking out the side. Tyler didn't seem to be throwing particularly hard, but that didn't mean anything. Sometimes a starter just saved it for the game.

What Matt did notice was that the Mets catcher hardly had to move his glove for any of the warm-up pitches once he set it behind the plate. If nothing else, this guy had solid control. Matt told himself to be ready to swing. Then he actually laughed to himself, because when didn't he go up there ready to swing?

"What's so funny?" Ben said.

Matt turned to him.

"Kind of laughing at a dumb thought I just had."

"Can't be about baseball."

"Actually, it was," Matt said. Then he said, "Ready to have some fun?"

Ben nodded out at the first-base coaching box.

"Maybe not as much as your mom," Ben said.

"You *think*?" Matt said.

Denzel hit the first pitch he saw for a single right over Tyler

Brewer's head. Denzel made a big turn, the way he always did, trying to maybe scare the Mets center fielder into rushing his throw back to the infield. But when the ball was back in the infield and he was back to the base, Matt could see his mom right next to Denzel, talking away and pointing. Denzel kept nodding as she did.

Yeah, Matt thought, *she is having herself some fun.*

She was *so* into this, just one batter into the game.

Matt looked up into the bleachers as he walked to the on-deck circle, and saw as many moms as there were dads. Maybe more. Why shouldn't more moms be on the field the way his was tonight?

José drew a walk.

First and second, nobody out.

Matt got into the box. This time the Mets catcher didn't say anything to him, just nodded as Matt gave his shin guards a tap with his bat.

Matt gave a quick look down at Sarge in the third-base coaching box. The only sign Sarge gave him was putting his fists together and making a swinging motion. Be a hitter. As if Matt had to be told. Then he gave a quick look down to his mom, who smiled and smacked the palms of her hands together, making a loud noise.

She really does look twelve, Matt told himself.

Then he focused on Tyler Brewer. With no outs, two on, and having just walked José, Matt knew he had to want to throw a strike in the worst way, not risk walking Matt and loading the bases for Big Ben. And when a pitcher was thinking that way—and Matt tried to think along with pitchers all the time—there was a good chance he might groove one.

Tyler grooved one.

The pitch was "middle in," as the announcers like to say.

Matt was all over it, almost too much. He covered the pitch so quickly with his bat that he was almost too far out in front and pulled it foul. But he didn't. The ball went screaming down the line before their third baseman could dive, on its way toward the sign for Franco's restaurant in the left field corner. Denzel scored easily. José went in to third base standing up. Matt did the same at second. Run in, still two runners on, still nobody out. The Astros had a great chance at a big inning. Now Matt was the one clapping his hands together.

Ben walked to the plate. Matt looked in at Ben and shook a fist, encouraging him. From third base he heard Sarge say, "Just get the barrel on it."

But Sarge's voice was quickly drowned out by Ben's dad.

"All you, big man!"

He was hanging over the fence, the way he usually did at Healey, almost even with first base tonight. Matt saw his mom turn at the sound of Mr. Roberson's voice before she focused all of her attention on Ben.

She didn't say anything to Ben. She hadn't said anything to Matt once he had been in the batter's box. But Matt could see from her face how much she wanted Ben to do well in this spot; how much she wanted him to get a hit. The infield was playing back. Ben didn't even need a clean hit to bring home another run, or even get the ball to the outfield. Just a ground ball to anybody except Tyler Brewer would do the job.

"*Give her a ride!*"

Ben swung and missed for strike one, swung so hard it was like he was trying to hit a six-run homer instead of a three-run homer.

Tyler threw the next pitch in the dirt. Before their catcher did a nice job blocking it, and holding José at third and Matt at second, Ben swung right over the pitch.

Sarge took a couple of steps toward the plate and said, "Just takes one, son."

Tyler threw the next pitch up in Ben's eyes, his biggest fastball of the inning. Ben showed his big leg kick, and did manage to get his bat on the ball. But the best he could do was a little pop fly right back to Tyler for the first out.

Then Stone lined out to the first baseman. The Astros still had two runners in scoring position. But now there were two

MIKE LUPICA

outs. Kyle struck out. The game stayed at 1–0. The Astros were ahead. They all felt they should have been ahead by more.

When Matt got back to the bench Ben started to say something, but stopped himself before simply reaching over and handing Matt his glove.

"Lot of baseball to be played tonight," Matt said, then ran out to second before he got a response.

The Mets scored two runs off Teddy in the top of the second. The Astros came right back with two of their own to take a 3–2 lead. The game kept going like that. By the top of the fifth, the Astros and Mets were tied 7–7. Both teams had their third pitcher of the game in there by then. Other than the top of the first, when Teddy had struck out the side, no pitcher had seen another one-two-three inning.

Ben led off the bottom of the fifth for the Astros. He had struck out twice by then, to go with the easy out he'd handed Tyler in the first. But this time, on the second pitch he saw from the Mets left-handed reliever, he blooped a single over the second baseman's head and into short right.

It wasn't much of a hit. It wasn't close to being a home run. But Ben was on first. He was the potential go-ahead run. Matt's mom was up on her toes, trying to come as close to Ben's ear as she could, talking away with her mouth and her hands, smiling as she did. Matt knew what she was telling him: Run hard on any ground ball. Play it halfway on a ball in the air to the outfield. If Stone hit a single to right, try to pick up Sarge as soon as possible, because Sarge would let him know whether or not to try for third. Just the basics. But always worth hearing, every time you were on base.

Matt's mom kept talking away while Stone dug in at the plate. Ben kept nodding.

Then he didn't go halfway on a ball that looked like it might be caught by the left fielder, but then fell in front of him. Matt heard his mom say, "Halfway." But either Ben didn't hear, or just froze as the ball came off Stone's bat, and when he did start running hard for second, it was too late. The left fielder threw the ball to the Mets second baseman for what should never have been a force play, but had become one.

Instead of first and second, nobody out, the Astros had Stone at first with one out. It had become a completely different inning, just like that.

As Ben ran back across the infield to the Astros' bench, head down, Matt heard what everybody heard:

"Not your fault, big man. You needed a coach there."

Matt couldn't believe it. Mr. Roberson had been closer to his mom than Matt was on the Astros' bench. If he hadn't heard her tell Ben to go halfway, he hadn't been listening.

She acted as if she hadn't heard. Maybe she didn't hear what

MIKE LUPICA

came next, maybe because Mr. Roberson managed to keep his voice down for a change.

"That's why she doesn't belong out there," he said.

Matt heard.

Then Matt was up off the bench and walking in Mr. Roberson's direction before he realized he was doing it, knowing exactly what he wanted to say, even though he knew his mom could fight her own battles.

This wasn't even a battle, Matt thought. This was just Mr. Roberson doing what Matt's mom called a "dumb-guy thing."

He was just going to tell Ben's dad that his mom belonged on this field as much as anybody.

But when he was in front of Mr. Roberson, he couldn't say anything.

"S-s-sh . . ."

She.

If he could just get that one word out, he knew the rest would follow right behind it.

He couldn't.

"What is it?" Mr. Roberson said. "Did Ben send you over here?"

Matt shook his head. He felt as if his tongue were stuck to his bottom teeth. He never wanted this to happen on a ball field and now it was happening to him again.

"S-s-sh . . ."

And this time, as ashamed as he felt, Matt gave up. He turned around to go back to the bench and nearly bumped into Ben, who leaned down and said, "I'm not finishing your sentence this time. Just starting one of my own."

Then in a voice quiet enough that Matt wondered if even the people behind Mr. Roberson in the bleachers could hear, Ben said, "It was my fault. Not Mrs. Baker's."

Then he turned back to Matt and said, "That wasn't for you. That was for me."

Matt and Ben sat back down on the bench and watched the guys at the bottom of the batting order keep getting hits until the Astros were back in front, 9–7. Sarge brought in Pat McQuade to close the game. But with two outs in the bottom of the sixth, Mike Clark dropped an easy fly ball in left. Just flat missed it. The kid who hit the ball ended up on second, and Pat walked the next batter. Then the guy who'd been the Mets' best hitter all night, their shortstop, doubled to right-center and the game was tied at nine all.

José was leading off for the Astros in the bottom of the sixth, then Matt, then Ben.

"Get us started," Matt said to José.

José grinned. "*Esta bien*," he said.

"Don't know that one," Matt said.

"It means 'alright,' dude," José said.

"Alright by me," Matt said.

José hit one hard to center, but it was right at the center fielder, and nothing more than a hard out. The left-handed reliever was still in there for the Mets. He got a fast strike on Matt, then missed away twice. He tried to go away with the fourth pitch of the sequence. It just wasn't far enough away and Matt went with the pitch, hitting a hard grounder to the left of their second baseman. The kid got to the ball in plenty of time, but the ball took a funny hop at the last second, hit off his glove, and rolled away from him toward the right field line. When Matt got to first, he saw his mom waving her arm and saying, "Go!" He cut the bag cleanly, took off for second, beat the second baseman's throw to the shortstop easily. His mom had taken a chance sending him. But she had read the play perfectly. When he looked over at her from second, she just winked at him.

Now Ben was the one with a chance to win the game.

Matt waited to hear something from Ben's dad, but didn't. He was standing in his same spot, arms crossed in front of him. But for once, he didn't say anything. All you heard was Matt's mom from the first base coaching box.

"Good swing, Ben," she said.

The first one he took wasn't. Big cut. Nothing but air. Same with the second pitch the left-hander threw him: big leg kick, even bigger swing than before, miss, strike two.

Ben shook his head, frustrated, asked the ump for time, stepped out of the box. Matt thought he might look over to where his dad was standing. He didn't. He stared down at Matt's mom.

She put her left foot just a little more forward than it was, and lightly tapped the grass in front of her.

The left-hander tried to come inside on Ben then. But this time there was no leg kick. There was hardly any movement at all to his front leg. Just a slight tap.

Matt was a few yards off second when the line drive went over him and over the shortstop in the direction of left-center. Matt waited until it came down, splitting the center-fielder and left-fielder.

By then Matt was on his way home with the run that won the game for the Astros, 10–9.

TWENTY-FOUR

There wasn't another game for the Astros until Saturday morning and only one practice scheduled before that. It wasn't nearly enough baseball for Matt and José. They felt as if they were playing hooky, but didn't want to be.

So they decided to meet Thursday afternoon on the back field at Healey Park and just work on stuff.

"What's the Spanish word for 'stuff'?" Matt asked.

José grinned.

"Stuff," he said.

"Are you messing with me again?" Matt asked.

"Probs," José said.

Before they went over to Healey, José had come to Matt's house for lunch. Matt's mom, who had majored in journalism in college, had started working at the South Shore *Dispatch*, the local paper, after Matt's dad left. She did a little bit of everything, editing and writing. She'd even helped to design the paper's website. But the best part of her job was that the editor-in-chief of the paper let her work from home as often as she needed to, so that she hardly ever had to have Mrs. Dudley, a retired schoolteacher who lived on their block, babysit for Matt. Matt hated it when she called Mrs. Dudley a babysitter. One time his mom had asked what she ought to call her and Matt said, "Mrs. Dudley."

So Matt's mom was home today and had made them sandwiches for lunch. As they were all cleaning up she said, "You know, I could come pitch to you guys if you want."

"You want to pitch *hardball*?" José asked.

As serious as José sounded, Matt smiled.

"Well," his mom said, "I know it will be a challenge for me. But I *will* need the two of you to show me the fine points of gripping the ball and throwing it accurately."

Now José looked at Matt.

"She's messing with me, isn't she?" he said.

"You picked up on that, huh?" Matt said.

When they got to the back field it was occupied by a dad pitching to a little boy who didn't appear to be more than four or five years old. When the dad saw Matt and his mom and José he said, "We're just wrapping up." Matt's mom told him to take as much time he needed. So they sat in the grass and watched the dad pitch underhand with a rubber ball that looked to be bigger than a baseball and smaller than a softball.

Every time the boy would connect, he'd go tearing around the bases, and his dad would say, "Another base hit for Christopher Marino!"

Matt and his mom and José started cheering and clapping every time Christopher connected. It made Matt remember being on this same field when he was about the same age Christopher was now, how excited he'd get when he'd put his bat on the ball.

He just hadn't had his dad pitching to him.

The truth was, he couldn't remember a time when his dad had ever pitched to him the way Christopher's dad was now. It had always been Matt's mom. He had no early baseball memories with his dad. Just her.

At one point Christopher's dad called over to them and said, "You mind if we go a few more minutes? My slugger here is on a roll."

Matt's mom said, "We're having more fun than he is."

Finally Christopher's dad announced that the bases were loaded with two outs in the bottom of the ninth of Game seven of the World Series and the game was tied.

"No pressure," José said to Matt.

"Our guy Christopher will be able to handle it, wait and see," Matt said.

The dad soft-tossed one last pitch. Christopher hit a line drive right back at him. The dad made a big show of diving out of the way as the ball rolled past him and into center field. Christopher was already tearing for first base as his dad got to his feet and chased after the ball, even if he wasn't chasing all that hard.

When he picked the ball up, Christopher had already turned for home. They could see Christopher was going to beat his dad to the plate easily. But he slid across the plate anyway, as his dad, laughing, dove for him in vain. Then Christopher was jumping to his feet and into the air, arms over his head, yelling "Grand slam," even though it sounded more like "*Gwand* slam."

His dad, covered in dirt the way Christopher was, picked up his son and held him high in the air.

"Put me down!" Christopher said, but didn't really seem to mean it.

He seemed to like the view from up there.

For some reason, in that moment Matt looked past Christopher and his dad, and all the way to the playground in the distance, beyond the right field fence.

And there, watching Christopher and his dad the same way Matt and his mom and José were, was Ben Roberson.

Before Matt could get his attention and wave him over, Ben got on his bike and rode away.

TWENTY-FIVE

Matt and José might not have had as much fun hitting against Matt's mom as Christopher had hitting against his dad.

But they all still had fun.

Matt and José insisted that she put the pitcher's screen in front of her, and she finally gave in.

"But I can still field my position," she said.

"We just don't want you to get hit by a comebacker and be lost for the season," Matt said.

"Especially since your season just started," José said.

"You guys are no fun," she said.

"Are too," Matt said.

Even there on the back field, she was coaching them. "Coaching them up good," as Sarge liked to say. It was as if she had just been waiting for a chance to coach guys their age. She had José try opening up his stance just slightly, as a way of helping him clear his hips. She had him raise his hands. She eventually sent both Matt and José to their infield positions and started hitting them ground balls. After that, she went down to first base and threw them grounders from there, so they could make their throws.

"This is more like practice than practice!" Matt called over to her at one point.

"Is that complaining I hear?" she said.

"Sounded more to me like whining," José said.

"Whose side are you on?" Matt said.

"Ours!" José said.

When they finished, they all sat back down in the grass near third base and drank water. Matt leaned back on his elbows and stared into the blue sky, unable to spot a cloud anywhere.

This had been a good idea. A good day.

But it bothered him that Ben could have been a part of it and wasn't, that he'd just up and left without even coming over to say hello.

He mentioned that now to his mom and José.

"Maybe he didn't see us," his mom said.

"He saw us, I know he did," Matt said, still staring up at the sky, feeling the sun on his face. "I just don't get him."

His mom said, "Maybe you need to make even more of an effort to get to know him better."

"Mom," Matt said. "I've tried."

"You mostly tried *here*," she said. "You tried when you tried to be his batting coach. Maybe the two of you could have a conversation about something other than his swing."

"He could make an effort too, you know," Matt said.

"Seems to me that he has, and more than once," she said. "First with that catcher, what's-his-name with the smart mouth, and then with his father."

She tilted her head at him, and grinned.

"You say you don't get him," she said. "But how well do you really know him?"

"I know he's really good at basketball and football," Matt said.

"Wow," she said. "Even I know that. But do you know what his dad does for a living?"

"No clue," Matt said.

"Same," José said.

"What about his mom?" Matt's mom asked. "She got a job?"

"Same answer," Matt said.

"Have you seen his mom at a game this season?" she said.

"Don't think so," Matt said. "But I don't even know what she looks like."

"I rest my case," his own mom said.

"Those aren't the kind of things guys talk about," Matt said.

He had rolled himself up into a sitting position, so he was facing her.

"I forgot about the law they passed saying that guys can only talk about sports and video games," she said.

"Not fair," Matt said. "You know that's not me."

"Well, it is me!" José said.

They laughed. But Matt's mom wasn't backing off this subject, or backing up.

"You are interested in more than baseball and video games," she said. "I know how curious you are. I saw how deep you dove into climate change when you did that paper this year. So how about doing that kind of deep dive with a would-be friend?"

"What if he doesn't want me to do that?" Matt said. "What if he likes things between us the way they already are?"

"You won't know until you try," she said. "And nobody I know tries harder at things, once he sets his mind to it, than you do."

Matt didn't say anything. But he knew she was right. His answer was to pull out his phone and send Ben a text and ask him if he wanted to hang out later.

A few seconds after he'd sent it he saw the little bubbles flashing that meant Ben was sending a reply.

Ur house or mine?

Now Matt hit him right back.

Mine. 3 o'clock ok?

Ben replied that it was. Matt told his mom and José that Ben was coming over in an hour. He told José that he was invited back to the house, too, but José said he told his mom he'd be home after the park.

"It's a good thing, anyway," José said. "This is between you and Ben."

"Not sure what 'this' is," Matt said.

"You'll make the right play," José said. "You always do, *nano*."

"*Nano?*"

"Combination of brother and friend," José said.

Matt looked at his mom.

"What if I don't know what to say?" he said.

"What did I tell you to do before?"

"Try," he said.

She winked at José now, and grinned.

"Can I coach, or what?" she said.

TWENTY-SIX

There was no reason for Matt to feel pressure about Ben coming over. But he was feeling it anyway.

And it was weird that he was even thinking about this, but he was worried about stuttering, even though he hardly ever stuttered inside his own house. To Matt, being inside his house was as safe as being inside his own brain, where he always spoke the way he wanted to, where the words really did come out like water from a faucet.

But he didn't want to stutter here today. Didn't want Ben to feel the kind of pressure Matt was feeling.

Stop it.

Ms. Francis was always telling him to imagine the best outcome for himself, not the worst. One time she said to him, "Do you ever see yourself making an error in a big spot in a game?"

He told her he never did.

"So that's the way you present yourself to your teammates, and even your opponents, correct?" she asked.

"Pretty much," Matt said.

"So do the same thing when you're not on a ball field," she said.

Matt heard the doorbell now, and yelled to his mom that he'd get it. Ben was standing there when he opened the door.

"Hey," Matt said.

"Hey."

As Matt waved him in, his mom came out of the kitchen, wiping her hands on the apron she was wearing. She'd already started tonight's dinner.

"Hi, Ben," she said."

"Hi, Mrs. Baker," he said. "It sure does smell good in there."

"Do you like pizza?" she said.

"Doesn't everybody?" Ben said.

"Well, you're welcome to stay," she said.

Ben thanked her, and said he'd call his dad later and ask him, and then he and Matt headed upstairs to Matt's room.

Once they were inside and Matt had closed the door, he didn't waste any time.

"I saw you at the park before," he said.

"I know," Ben said.

"You should have stuck around," Matt said. "My mom ended up pitching BP to José and me."

Ben managed a grin. "Everybody knows I can't hit your mom's pitching," he said.

"The last thing she wanted to do was strike you out," Matt said. "You know that, right?"

"Trust me," Ben said, "the last thing I wanted was to *get* struck out."

Matt sat cross-legged on his bed. Ben was sitting in the swivel chair at Matt's desk. They just stared at each other, as if waiting for the other to make the first move.

"This might not be easy," Matt's mom had said before Ben got there. "But do the best you can, because you might not get another crack at this."

"What if I don't know what to say?" Matt said.

"Then listen to what he has to say," she said.

For now, there was just all this awkward silence between

them. When Matt couldn't take it any longer he said, "You want to play Xbox or something?"

He couldn't believe *those* words had gotten out of his mouth. He'd never liked playing video games. He'd always preferred real games.

"Not much into that stuff," Ben said.

As soon as he did, Matt blew out some air, relieved.

"Good!" he said. "Me neither."

"Why did you ask?"

Matt laughed and said, "I have no idea!"

But at least they had something in common besides baseball. Maybe it was a start. But then came another silence, longer than the one before.

Ben was the one who broke it this time.

"It was kind of cool today," he said, "watching that kid with his dad. I can still remember my dad taking me to the park when I was little."

Matt laughed again.

"You were never little," he said.

"You know, you're right," Ben said. "Even when I was little I was already big."

"My dad left when I was about the same age as that little boy," Matt said.

"Yeah, but at least you've got a cool mom," Ben said.

"I still always wonder what it would be like to have both parents around the way you do," Matt said.

Ben turned slightly in his chair, and looked out the window. When he turned back he said, "Not anymore."

Now Matt really didn't know what to say.

Ben saved him.

"My mom is the one who left," he said.

More than ever, Matt knew that he had to be a good listener. But first he said, "I'm sorry. I didn't know."

"Do you *want* to know?" Ben said.

"If you want me to," Matt said.

Now Ben was the one blowing out some air.

"She just finally got tired of the fighting," he said. "At the end, they were fighting all the time. He'd say, 'Nobody made you marry me.' And she'd come back with, 'You're not the man I married.'"

Matt waited.

"She'd tell him that he was so obsessed with being a guy's guy that he'd forgotten how to be a good man," Ben said.

Ben leaned back in the chair and rubbed his eyes hard with both hands.

"But my dad kept going back to how she knew who she was marrying," he said. "And she'd come right back and tell him she didn't know the person he'd become. That he was somebody else, and that she didn't want him to turn me into that somebody else."

"I'm sorry," Matt said again.

"When they'd bring me into it, I'd start to think I was the problem," Ben said. "But I knew the problem was them."

"My mom always told me that my dad leaving had nothing to do with her, or with me," he said. "It was all about him."

Ben nodded.

"There was no place for me to go in our house where I couldn't hear them yelling at each other," he said.

"I . . . I . . ."

Matt wasn't stuttering. He just didn't know what to say.

Ben waited. They both did. Finally Ben said, "I don't want to jam you up by finishing your sentence."

"The only thing jamming me up," Matt said, "is not knowing how to help."

"You're helping me by just hearing me out," Ben said. "I'll be fine. My dad says we just have to man up until she comes to her senses."

Ben smiled, even though he didn't look very happy.

"But then, maybe my mom already *has* come to her senses," he said.

"I had no idea any of this was going on," Matt said. "You

seem to be in a good mood most of the time."

"Nobody except my dad and me know," Ben said.

"Is your mom still in South Shore?"

Ben shook his head. "She went to stay with my aunt in Florida."

"Maybe you shouldn't tell her what he said about manning up," Matt said.

"That's just my dad being my dad," Ben said.

There was one more silence, until Ben said, "I really did need to talk about this with somebody. And you seem like a good guy, I guess."

Matt grinned. "Thanks," he said. "I guess."

He thought about asking Ben if he wanted to go throw a ball around in the backyard. But decided not to. This wasn't about being teammates today. Just the two of them trying to figure out a way to be friends.

Or maybe they already had.

TWENTY-SEVEN

The Astros beat the Scofield Pirates in Scofield on Saturday. Matt hit the ball on the nose every time up, but came away with nothing to show for that except four hard outs. But the team won. Ben struck out a couple of times but also got a sharp single to left his last time up. He hadn't shortened up his swing that Matt could tell. But he'd lost the leg kick for the time being. And the best thing about the hit was it came with two runners in scoring position and two outs. For once

Ben didn't try to hit the ball clear out of sight. He just went with an outside pitch to right field, and got the two runs home.

He also didn't have his dad in his ear, or anybody else's. After the game, when Matt asked Ben where his father was, Ben said, "A meeting."

"On a Saturday?" Matt asked.

"Yeah," Ben said, and left it at that, and so did Matt.

"Solid at bat last time up," Matt said.

"Didn't try to do too much," he said.

"And a lot happened," Matt said.

"Yeah."

"I should have made a lot more happen today than I did," Matt said.

"Are you serious?" Ben said. "You scorched the ball every time up."

"Outs are outs," Matt said. "That's the way I look at things, anyway."

"Any time you want to trade swings, fine with me," Ben said.

"Listen," Matt said. "My swing is mine. Yours is yours. Maybe we just learned differently, is all. Maybe I'd be a totally different player if I were as big as you."

"You don't want to be me right now," he said. "Trust me."

They were at the fence behind what had been their bench on the third-base side of Scofield Park, backs to the field, in front of the small bleachers where the Astros parents who'd made the trip to Scofield had sat.

By now the bleachers were completely empty.

"Wish my dad could have seen that hit," Ben said. "Baseball's about the only thing that makes him happy these days."

Their next game was on Tuesday night, at home.

It was always the same during baseball season, especially the summer All-Stars season. It was as if Matt wasn't on Daylight Savings Time. He was only on baseball time. The only days that mattered to him on the calendar were the ones when he had a game. His mom had even colored in game days on their kitchen calendar, in bright yellow. She would put a W and the score if the Astros won, a much smaller L and the score when they lost.

So far there was only that one L, from the Cubs game.

This week Matt met with Ms. Francis on Monday afternoon. As always, he talked about things that had happened to him since their last session. Today he told her about Ben coming to his house and what Ben had told him. Matt talked about what Mr. Roberson said about his mom being a coach, and how Matt had locked up tight when he'd tried to defend her.

"Not that she needed me to defend her," Matt said.

"Sounds like she didn't even know what you were about to defend her *for*," Ms. Francis said.

"Then Ben defended me," Matt said. "Again."

"Tell me," she said.

Matt did. The words came easily to him. They usually did in here. Sometimes he felt as safe here as he did in his own house. Sometimes he thought he was better talking about himself than he was talking for himself. It was a lot like when he'd do baseball play-by-play alone in his room. He could talk all night in there.

"Sounds like it's harder for Ben with his dad than you thought, or than he's willing to admit to you," Ms. Francis said.

"Really hard."

"But there's a part of him who steps in when he sees that things are hard for you," she said. "That's what friends do."

"It's funny," Matt said. "In my brain, I always thought he had enough friends."

She smiled. "Looks can be deceiving."

"I always thought that being big made things easy for him," Matt said. "Maybe it's not all people make it out to be. Being big, I mean."

"Which people?" she said. She was still smiling at him.

"Me, I guess."

"When you and Ben were talking in your room, even though it sounds like he was doing most of the talking, did you stutter one time?"

He told her no, that the closest he'd come was when he couldn't find something to say that would make Ben feel better about things.

"Do you think he did feel better about things after you two played catch and he went home?" she said.

"Think so," Matt said.

"That's pretty big stuff, if you ask me."

"I was thinking after he left that I don't have a dad in my life and he doesn't have a mom, at least for now," Matt said.

She said, "Maybe you two have way more in common than you knew before he came over."

Then Ms. Francis said, "And maybe things that you think are huge problems in your life really aren't."

"Like being small," he said. "And stuttering."

"Maybe," she said, "when you find yourself worrying about somebody else you don't worry as much about all that."

TWENTY-EIGHT

Tuesday's game was against the Sherrill Mariners.

Last year in All-Stars, the South Shore guys had played a great, extra-inning game against them in the league semifinals, Denzel finally scoring the winning run on a wild pitch after he'd tripled in the bottom of the eighth.

"They're still bad dudes," Denzel said when they'd finished with their pregame drills.

"We're still badder," Kyle said.

"And how are you so sure that our best is still better than their best?" Matt asked him.

Kyle grinned. "Analytics!" he said.

"First of all," José said, "we all know you have no interest in analytics."

"And," Matt said, "there's no such thing as analytics for Little League."

"Thank the lord," Matt's mom said from behind them.

They all laughed. Some nights, Matt thought, it even felt more awesome than usual that they had a game to play. Tonight was just one of those nights. Maybe Ms. Francis was right. Sometimes you had to remind yourself that you were probably a lot better off than you thought. Even if you were the smallest guy on the team.

Even if you stuttered.

Even if one of your parents had left a long time ago.

There was another reason Matt was a little more excited than usual about the Astros–Mariners game: His mom was head coach tonight. They'd found out a few minutes after they'd arrived at the field. Sarge had been away in business in Boston, and called from the road saying he was caught in horrible traffic and probably wouldn't even be back in South Shore until the game was over.

Now she gathered the Astros around her before Mike Clark

went out to throw the first pitch of the game.

"Okay," she said, "you guys have one job tonight, and that's to make me look good in front of the other parents."

"Is that what they call peer pressure, Mrs. B.?" José said.

"Totally!" she said. "If I mess this game up, maybe no woman will ever get another chance to coach in this league."

"Being dramatic there, Mom?" Matt said.

"Little bit," she said.

Ben's dad was back, but Matt hadn't heard anything from him during warm-ups, not even during batting practice, when he would usually start in with his cheerleading for Ben. He wasn't even at his usual spot, leaning over the fence near first base. He was seated by himself, down past first, in the lawn chair he'd brought.

Somehow sitting in the chair made him look even bigger than he actually was. Matt could barely see the chair underneath him.

"How's your dad doing?" Matt said to Ben.

"He's fine," Ben said. "He promised me that he'll keep his voice down tonight. But I guess we'll see."

Ben gave a look over his shoulder to where his dad was sitting in his chair.

"I just want him to be happy," he said.

Matt thought it was supposed to be the other way around,

that parents were supposed to worry more about their kids being happy. But he didn't say that. He just reached over and pounded Ben some fist.

Mike Clark got out of a bases-loaded jam in the top of the first, finally striking out the Mariners catcher on a 3-2 pitch. Then in the bottom of the inning, Denzel singled, José flied out to left, Matt walked.

First and second, one out, for Ben.

If Ben's dad was going to make some noise, now was the time. But he didn't say anything.

Crickets, as Matt's mom liked to say.

Maybe he was going to keep his promise to Ben and keep his thoughts to himself tonight.

Matt's mom was coaching third tonight. Denzel's dad was in the first-base coaching box. Ben stepped to the plate against Tommy O'Neill, who'd been Sherrill's best pitcher last summer.

And just like that, Ben's leg kick was back, his front leg up there as high as ever. Tommy came at him with a high fastball and Ben swung underneath it, missing by a lot. Matt looked across the infield at his mom. But she was watching Ben.

"Good swing," she said.

She meant the next one. Because the last one hadn't been anything close to the swing she'd suggested to him, the one that had plated the Astros' last two runs in the Pirates game.

Maybe, Matt thought, this was Ben's dad swing.

Now he used it again and swung and missed at strike two, the ball even more up in Ben's eyes than the first pitch from Tommy had been.

But he managed to make contact on the next pitch, and hit a high pop fly to short right field, maybe twenty feet behind the infield dirt. The Mariners second baseman raced back, got underneath it, and they could all hear him calling off his right fielder.

Matt did what you're supposed to: got himself far enough off first that he could get back easily when the second baseman caught the ball, but close enough to second that he could beat a throw if the guy somehow dropped it. Denzel, he saw, did the same thing between second and third.

They were both in the right spots when the second baseman *did* drop the ball.

Maybe he had a little too much time waiting for the ball to come down. Matt knew he felt that way sometimes—too many thoughts inside his head, imagining all the players in the game and all the fans staring at him.

Now they were staring at the Mariners second baseman as the ball hit off the heel of his glove and fell to the side.

The bases were going to be loaded for the Astros with just one out.

"*First!*" he heard the Mariners first baseman yell from behind him.

Matt was in to second by then. Denzel was in to third. So why was the first baseman yelling for the ball?

Because Ben hadn't run the ball out.

He was only halfway between home and first, his bat still in his hand, only just now starting to run hard, having assumed the ball he'd hit in the air was a sure out. And when he did start running, it was too late, by a lot. He was out. By a lot.

Stone hit a fly ball to left that would have been an easy sacrifice fly and gotten the Astros at least one run. But it was just the third out of the inning.

When Matt's mom made it back across the field from third base, she went right to Ben and said, "Talk to you for a second?"

He made room so she could sit next to him at the end of the bench. He already had his first baseman's mitt on his left hand. But he had his head down. He had to know what he'd done. Announcers talked all the time on TV about guys running their teams out of innings. Now Ben had *not* run his team out of a potential big first inning.

He also had to know he had broken one of Sarge's few rules of baseball, about always running balls out, no matter what. Matt knew his mom knew that rule too, because she had heard it along with all the other parents on the first night the Astros practiced as a team.

Matt's teammates were already on their way out to the field. Matt stayed behind, kneeling down to tie his shoes, wanting to hear what happened next; wanting to see how his mom was going to handle this on her first night of being a head coach.

"I don't have to tell you Sarge's rule, do I?" Matt's mom said to Ben.

"No, ma'am," he said.

"So you know that if you don't run a ball out, you have to come out of the game, right?" she said.

"Yes, ma'am," Ben said. He looked up at her. Matt wasn't even sure Ben knew he was taking off his mitt. "Sarge says there's never an excuse for not hustling, not in the big leagues, not in Little League."

"There's more to baseball than hitting," Matt's mom said, still keeping her voice low. "We both know that."

"Yes, ma'am," Ben said.

He sounded like a little boy.

"And we both know that this won't happen again," Matt's mom said. "But for tonight, you take the rest of the game off." She turned to Pat McQuade, who in addition to being the team's closer was Ben's backup at first base. It's why he always brought his regular glove to the game, plus a first baseman's mitt of his own. "Patrick, why don't you go out there and take over for Ben at first?"

She turned back to Ben and smiled and said, "You be a good teammate the rest of the night."

Ben had forgotten to take off his batting helmet. She gave it a light rap with her knuckles and walked down to the other end of the bench.

She had just sat down when they heard Ben's dad behind them.

"Wait a second!" he shouted. "You're taking him out?"

Matt was just now on his way back out to second. He turned and saw Mr. Roberson come out of his lawn chair and walk fast in the direction of the Astros' bench.

And Matt's mom.

"You can't take him out," Ben's dad said.

Matt's mom turned to look at him. But then, everybody at Healey Park was looking at him now.

"You're not the coach of this team!" Mr. Roberson said, his voice rising a little more.

Matt's mom stood now, and began walking over to where Mr. Roberson was standing on his side of the fence. Matt knew his mom. He knew how much she hated loud voices. She had told him once that her own father had been too loud, because of a bad temper. She never yelled at Matt. She hated drama, and she hated scenes. The kind of scene that Ben's dad was making now.

Matt walked a little closer to them and heard his mom say, "I'm the coach tonight."

"You wouldn't take your own son out of the game for making one mistake on the bases," Mr. Roberson said.

"First of all, I would," she said. "And my son knows I would. And second of all, I don't appreciate being yelled at this way."

"And I don't appreciate what you just did to *my* son," he said. "Not that I signed up to have a . . ."

Somehow they all heard him stop himself before he said he hadn't signed up to have a woman coach his son's baseball team.

". . . to have somebody other than Sarge coach this team," is the way he finished the sentence.

"I'm only doing what Sarge would have done if he'd been here," Matt's mom said. "You were at the practice when he told us all his rule about the consequences of not running out balls. It's part of being on this team. It's Sarge's rule, not mine."

"Dad," Ben said.

He had walked over and was standing behind Matt's mom.

"Shut up, Ben," Mr. Roberson said.

Then he turned back to Matt's mom and said, "Mike hasn't thrown a pitch yet. So Ben is technically still in the game. So put him back in."

At this point Matt saw the home plate umpire walking up the first base line, clearly having heard enough. Or seen enough. Or both.

"I'm afraid I can't do that," Rachel Baker said.

Standing her ground. His mom.

Standing tall, if you thought about it.

"You're being an idiot," Mr. Roberson said. His face was very red. His voice was still very loud.

"One of us is," Matt's mom said.

"So you're telling me Ben's out of this game?" Mr. Roberson said.

"You both are," the home plate umpire said.

"Wait a second," Mr. Roberson said. "You're telling *me* to leave?"

"Yes sir," the ump said. "And if you leave, and that means leave quietly, none of this will extend beyond tonight's game."

"You think you have the right to do that?"

"I know I do, sir, and so does the other umpire and so do the two coaches," the ump said. "Now, I am asking you as respectfully as possible to leave and let the kids finish the game, which happens to be what the night is supposed to be about."

Mr. Roberson opened his mouth, then closed it. He looked at Matt's mom again. He looked at the ump. Finally he looked at Ben and said, "Let's go."

Don't do it, Matt thought.

Matt tried to call out his name. He just wanted to say, "Ben, stop." He wanted to tell him to stay.

But he couldn't get the words out, even though he knew this was important, even if this was Ben's dad giving him an order, he knew it was important for Ben to stay and be a part of the team. Ben couldn't control how his dad was acting. Just how he was about to act.

Ben put his head back down and walked to his right, toward the gate. Then he went through the gate and over to his dad, who by then had gone to fold up his lawn chair. The two of them walked in the direction of the parking lot. Mr. Roberson, Matt saw, tried to put an arm around Ben's shoulder. Ben moved away from him far enough that he couldn't.

The next thing anybody heard at Healey Park was the home plate ump saying, "Play ball."

Then he added, "Finally."

At second base, only loud enough for himself to hear, Matt finally said, "Ben, stop."

Just too late, for both of them.

TWENTY-NINE

The Astros ended up winning the game. Pat McQuade, who didn't just replace Ben at first but in the cleanup spot as well, got a big double with two outs in the bottom of the fifth and the bases loaded, scoring Denzel and José and Matt as the Astros were breaking the game wide open.

Matt ended the game with a neat diving stop to his left, covering himself with dirt in the process, throwing out the Mariners third baseman from his knees. Nothing better than not only winning the game, Matt thought, but ending it with the dirtiest uniform on the field.

It just didn't feel quite as good as it normally would have, because of what had happened all the way back in the first inning with Ben's dad.

Matt's mom addressed the team almost as soon as the game was over. It was right after she'd thanked the home plate umpire for the way he'd handled the situation.

Some of the Astros players sat on their bench. Some stood behind it. Some sat on the grass in front of it. Matt's mom walked up and down in front of them, still keeping her voice down. This wasn't for the benefit of the parents. This was for the Astros.

"I'm truly sorry about what happened with Ben," she said. "But I am not going to apologize for my decision to pull him from the game. I'll say it again: He knows Sarge's rules, you guys know them, I know them. Your parents all know them. Respecting his rules is another way of respecting the game."

Matt gave a quick look around. She had their attention, the way she always had Matt's when something important was being discussed.

"And I can promise you that what I told Ben's dad is true," she said. "If it had been Matt who'd done it, he would have been coming out of the game too."

MIKE LUPICA

She stopped now, clasped her hands together, put them under her chin. That usually meant she was wrapping things up.

She smiled.

"Sooooooo," she said, "there was a lot going on tonight. But what I want you guys to remember is what happened on the field, not off it. Just about everybody on our team did something to help us win tonight." She pulled her hands apart and clapped them loudly in front of her. "And the best part is, I didn't do anything to mess you up!"

José was seated next to Matt on the bench. He raised his hand.

"Well," he said, "you did send me home on that ball that Kyle hit in the sixth and I got thrown out."

"Zip it, José!" she said.

They all laughed.

If you added it all up, Matt thought, it *had* been a pretty good night for the team.

Just not everybody on it.

When they got home Matt asked his mom if she thought he should text Ben or call him to see how he was doing.

"I'd give him some room, just for tonight," she said. "I'm sure he's embarrassed. Give him a chance to put a little distance between himself and what happened."

"He and his dad both have a lot going on," Matt said.

"I may have mentioned this once or twice in your life," she said. "But being a parent isn't for the faint of heart."

"Mr. Roberson was there the night Sarge told everybody what he expected from us this season," Matt said. "So why did he act that way with you?"

"I don't think he cared about any of that in the moment," she said. "He thought he was looking out for his kid, but he just couldn't get out of his own way."

"You're being pretty nice about it," Matt said.

They were at the kitchen table eating ice cream.

"This may sound silly," she said, "but I pride myself on being a nice person. And you can't pick your spots with that. You know what I always tell you, champ. You're supposed to do the right thing, whether everybody is watching or nobody is watching."

"But you didn't back down," Matt said.

She winked at him. "No, I did not."

"Mr. Roberson found out how tough you are," he said to her.

She stood up. They'd both cleaned their bowls. She picked them both up.

"Wasn't doing that for him," she said. "I was doing that for me."

She went up to her room to watch another TV show with

English accents. Ben went to his to watch baseball on his laptop. The Astros were playing the Yankees at Yankee Stadium. Almost as soon as he had the game on his screen, Aaron Judge hit a ball to right field that the announcers thought might be a home run. But Judge, Matt noticed, took nothing for granted. He ran hard out of the box, and ended up with a stand-up double.

When he got to second base, he was standing next to José Altuve.

The television camera did a close-up on the two of them, and Matt thought Judge looked even more than a foot taller than Altuve. Two of the best players in baseball. Two guys who had finished first and second that time in the MVP voting. And one of them looked like a giant and one of them looked like he was twelve years old.

Judge leaned down and said something to Altuve. Altuve smiled and patted Judge on the back with his glove. He said something back. Judge smiled. They were just speaking baseball with each other. They both wanted to win the game, obviously. But in that moment, they both looked as happy to be playing as if they were both Little Leaguers.

Matt wished things had been like that tonight for the biggest guy on his team.

After the third out for the Yankees, he turned the volume

on his laptop down all the way, so he could no longer hear the announcers. He was going to quietly do some play-by-play. Matt knew he didn't really have to keep his voice down. His mom knew by now that if she heard him talking he wasn't talking to himself, just to baseball.

Altuve was leading off the top of the third for the Astros.

But alone in his room, his favorite player in the world digging in at home plate, Matt was suddenly stuck. It never happened when he was alone like this with a game. It was happening now.

He opened his mouth, all right. But nothing came out.

Altuve put a charge into one, and sent a home run high over the left field wall.

Matt opened his mouth again.

Nothing.

He finally closed his laptop, got up, washed up and brushed his teeth, shut off his bedroom light, and got under the covers, even though it was way earlier than his usual bedtime, even in the summer.

But all he could see after he closed his eyes was Ben standing there while his dad made that scene, and then following his dad to the parking lot.

Throughout the whole thing, all Ben had said was one word: "Dad."

It was almost as if Ben were the one at the front of the line at the ice cream truck, with no place to go.

No place to hide.

Matt had always thought of baseball as safe place. Not for Ben. Not tonight.

THIRTY

He waited until the next morning to send Ben a text, asking him if he wanted to hang out again, not mentioning everything that had happened at the game.

No reply.

"Give him some room," his mom had said. "Don't crowd him." Matt knew that if he sent another text or called—or even just rode over to Ben's house on his bike—that would be crowding him big-time.

José was already at Matt's house by the time Matt had texted Ben. José's parents had gone into the city and didn't want to leave him alone. So he was going to spend the day with Matt. Matt's mom had told José's parents not to rush back, she was inviting him to dinner too.

"You can't just stare at your phone all day," José said to Matt. "Ben's probably doing fine."

"The other times I've texted him, he hit me back pretty quickly," Matt said.

"Maybe," José said, "he just doesn't feel like talking." He tilted his head at Matt, and grinned. "Dude, I *know* you can relate to that."

"All of a sudden," Matt said, "I feel like I spend more time talking—or talking about talking—than I do playing baseball!"

"Guy just needs his space," José said.

"You sound like my mom," Matt said.

"It's like she always says," José said. "Can she coach or what?"

They talked about riding their bikes into town and seeing an afternoon showing of the new *Avengers* movie, but then decided it was way too nice out for that. But then they decided to do what they both knew they'd wanted to do all along:

Go over to Healey, just the two of them, and play baseball.

"We won't have my mom to pitch to us today," Matt said.

"So I'll pitch to you if we want to hit and you can pitch to me," José said.

Matt's mom was spending a few hours at the *Dispatch* office. When Matt texted her to tell her that he and José were heading over to the park, she did respond right away:

But I want to come out and play!

Matt answered by asking if she wanted him to send pics of them playing. This reply came more quickly than the first:

Now you're just being mean

Healey was close enough to the house that Matt and José could have walked over. But they had bats and gloves and a bag of balls and water bottles, so it was easier to take their bikes.

When they got there they saw that they had the back field to themselves. They started out just soft-tossing, slowly moving farther away from each other until José was out in deep center field and Matt was standing at home plate. And even with that kind of distance between them, Matt barely had to move for the ball. It was because José had some arm. Sometimes in a game when José had to make a throw from the hole, Matt thought

José threw the ball harder than the pitchers in the game.

"I know I've told you this before," Matt yelled out to him after another throw home, "but you should totally pitch."

"My father was a shortstop when he was a boy in Santo Domingo," José yelled back. "So was his father. We think of shortstop as our family business."

When they were ready to hit, they came up with a game they called line drive derby. Sarge said trying to hit home runs, even for a home run hitter like Ben, only screwed up your swing. So today Matt and José came up with a scoring system for line drives: You got three points for a line drive to left, right, or center. You got four points for any ball that made it all the way to the wall.

You only got one point if you hit a ball that cleared the wall.

Matt finally won, coming from two points down, last time up, when he hit one to right-field that one-hopped the wall.

"It was like you drained a three-pointer to win a basketball game," José said.

"My mom always taught me to use the whole field," Matt said.

"Seems to me she taught you a lot more than that," José said.

"What's the Spanish word for star?" Matt asked.

"*Estrella,*" José said.

"My mom," Matt said, "is the real *estrella* in our house."

They flopped down in the grass and were drinking water when they heard, "Hey, look. It's the little dude."

Mat turned around, but had already recognized the voice.

It belonged to Joey.

The Glenallen catcher with the big mouth.

THIRTY-ONE

Joey was halfway between first base and the right field wall, so there was some distance between him and where Matt and José sat in the grass near home plate.

But they could hear him fine.

"If we ignore him," José said, only loud enough for Matt to hear, "do you think he'll go away?"

"Doubtful," Matt said.

It was getting to where he hated loud voices and loud people as much as his mom did.

Joey was with another boy about his same size, whom Matt didn't recognize. Now the two of them were walking past the bench on the first-base side of the back field, toward home plate.

Joey had a big smile.

"Hey, little dude, remember me?" Joey said.

How could I forget?

They walked through the small opening in the gate behind the bench. Joey actually looked smaller than he did in catcher's gear. But his voice, his attitude, were as big as ever.

There was clearly no way to ignore them, so José said, "What are you doing in town?"

"This is my cousin Sam," Joey said, as if that was all the explanation they deserved.

Matt didn't say anything.

"Still not talking to me?" Joey said to him.

José stood up and said to Matt, "Let's go." He reached down and began tossing their old baseballs into the bag. Matt stood and helped him.

He thought of one of his mom's favorite expressions: "Do not engage." He told himself to be as cool with Joey as his mom had been with Mr. Roberson.

By now Joey was only a few feet away from them. His cousin

still hadn't said a word, or acted as if he wanted to be a part of this, whatever *this* was.

"Sam and I were thinking about getting some ice cream from that truck over there," Joey said. "But then I see two guys playing ball, and when I get closer, I realize one of them is my friend, the little dude from the Astros."

He turned to his cousin Sam. "He's the one I told you about, who said he got hit by a pitch even though he didn't."

"The ump said he did," José said.

José was speaking for Matt. Matt was happy to let him.

"The ump's not around now to protect him," Joey said.

They'd finished putting the balls in the bag while Joey kept talking. Their bikes were leaning against the fence. *All we have to do*, Matt thought, *is walk over there, get on them, ride away.*

Joey grinned.

"W-w-what's the matter, little d-d-dude?" he said. "You don't want to talk to me? Or you c-c-can't?"

There it was.

He knew what had happened during their game.

He *knew.*

Joey laughed, as if cracking himself up.

No one *Matt* knew made fun of his stuttering. No one made fun of him, in class or on the Astros, when he couldn't get the words out. But now Joey was.

"C-c-cat got your tongue?" Joey said.

Matt was holding the ball bag in one hand. José was holding their bats and gloves. Matt dropped the bag now, and moved a little closer to Joey than they already were.

When he spoke, the words came right out of him. He could even feel himself smiling.

"Want to take a swing?" he said.

"A swing at you?" Joey said. He shook his head. "Can't. I only pick on guys my own size."

He waited. So did Matt. Maybe this one time, he wanted someone to think that he was stuck.

But he wasn't.

"No," he said finally. "I mean swing a bat. I pitch to you. One at bat. Then you pitch to me. Longest ball wins."

Now he wanted to play Home Run Derby.

"You're not a pitcher," Joey said. "Neither am I."

But Matt could see something in his eyes. Maybe he wasn't so sure of himself now. So sure he could back up his big talk.

"If I'm not a pitcher," Matt said, "it ought to be easy for you to take me deep." He nodded at José. "You can use my bat, or my friend's."

"C'mon," Joey's cousin Sam said. "Let's do this."

Suddenly it was Joey who had no place to go.

"I'll go first," he said.

José handed him both bats. Joey swung one, then the other. José's, Matt knew, was a little heavier. Joey went with that one.

"Your cousin can call balls and strikes," Matt said. "José will catch. Three strikes and you're out."

He turned and walked out to the pitcher's mound, feeling as if he'd won something here already, because he hadn't choked on his own words, not in front of this guy. Not even after the guy had made fun of him.

José went into his crouch behind the plate, and called out to Matt, "You need any warm-up pitches?"

"Nope," Matt said.

Sarge always said people were surprised, when Matt would put a charge into a ball, how much power he had, because of his lack of size. But only Matt's teammates knew, because he only had to make a short throw from second base most of the time, how strong his arm was. Sometimes he could show it off when he had to make a relay throw to the plate from short right field, but not very often.

When he had to, though, Matt could throw what the announcers called peas.

He got his arm from his mom.

Joey took a few fast, hard practice swings.

"You good?" Matt said.

"Bring it," Joey said.

Matt poured a fastball past him for strike one. Joey was late on the pitch and swung underneath it, trying to end the game between them, at least in his mind, with one swing of José's bat.

José stayed in his crouch, hardly having had to move his glove, and fired the ball back to Matt.

Matt took a short windup and threw another high, hard fastball past Joey, the ball making a sweet popping sound in José's glove.

Two strikes.

Joey stepped out. He didn't look at Matt, just over at his cousin. "This one is mine," he said.

Nah, Matt thought.

You're mine.

Matt gave Joey time to step back in, take his stance. He didn't want him complaining that Matt had quick-pitched him, that he wasn't ready.

Matt took some air in, let it out. It was an exercise to relax himself that Ms. Francis had taught him. Count to four as you take the breath in, hold it for four, let it out the same way.

Then he threw the next pitch as hard as he'd ever thrown a baseball in his life, right down the middle. But it didn't matter. Joey had no chance. He took his biggest cut yet. Missed.

Strike three.

Matt didn't say anything. Neither did Joey. Nothing *to* say.

Joey might act like a jerk. But he was a player, too, and knew he'd just gotten beaten, badly.

Matt walked to the plate. Joey went to the pitcher's mound. Matt handed him his glove and the ball and went to get his own bat. José stayed behind the plate. José asked if Joey wanted any warm-up pitches.

"Don't need any," he said.

Matt remembered from the Glenallen game that Joey had a pretty good arm himself. There had been a pitch that briefly got away from him and Denzel, on first base, had taken off for second. Because of Denzel's speed, Joey shouldn't have had a chance to throw him out, but nearly did.

Matt nodded at Joey to let him know he was ready. Joey went into a short windup of his own and came with his own high, hard heat.

And Matt hammered the ball.

To dead center.

No sound in José's glove this time. Just the sound of the ball on the sweet part of Matt's bat. If this had been a real game, Matt would have been running hard out of the box. But this was a different kind of game. All he had to do was watch the flight of the ball, same as Joey was after he'd turned to watch. But he *was* a player. He was a catcher. He knew that sound.

All four of them watched as the ball disappeared over the center field fence.

Matt turned to José and jerked his head toward the bikes. José nodded. He was the one who walked out to the mound to collect Matt's glove. Matt already had the ball bag over his shoulder.

It was one ball lighter than when they'd shown up.

Joey was still standing on the mound.

"Aren't you going to say anything?" he called out to them.

Matt didn't turn back. He just shook his head. José had the bat bag over his shoulder, with their gloves inside. Matt stuck the ball bag into the basket on the front of his bike. The two of them rode away. They didn't hear another word from Joey.

Maybe the cat got his tongue.

THIRTY-TWO

The Astros won their next game, and the one after that. Then the one after that. Suddenly they were 11–1 in their fourteen-game regular season. The postseason tournament to decide the league champion was simple enough after that: The top four teams made it. The top seed played the fourth seed in the semis, the second seed played the third. Then the championship game.

By now the Astros had won their rematch with the Cubs, the

only team to have beaten them. They beat the Glenallen Giants again, with hardly any chirp out of Joey. He called Matt "little dude" on Matt's first trip to the plate in that one, but his heart didn't seem to be in it.

Everything that needed to be said between them had already been said. At least Matt hoped so. He'd always wanted to let his play do the talking, and not just with a guy like Joey.

Ben Roberson had never mentioned what had happened that night with his dad, not one time. Not in practice, not when the Astros were winning their next several games. It was as if it had never happened, even though they all knew it had. Ms. Francis liked to talk about bells that couldn't be unrung. But it seemed Ben sure was trying to unring a big one.

But what he *wasn't* trying to do, as far as Matt could tell, was be anything more than Matt's teammate.

They were back to being teammates, not friends.

Ben hadn't stopped talking to Matt. If you didn't know, you wouldn't have thought things changed between them. But they had. Ben never asked if Matt wanted to hang out. As a result, Matt didn't ask Ben to hang out. Ben was still trying to hit baseballs over the wall. But he had built a different kind of wall around himself. At least that was the way Matt looked at it.

Ben's dad had managed to turn down the volume at Astros games. He didn't talk to Matt's mom. He didn't talk to Sarge.

Once he arrived at Healey Park, or at some road field, he really didn't talk to anybody except Ben, whom he kept telling to give the ball a ride, just not quite as loudly as before.

This deep into the season, things were pretty much the way they had been at the start: Matt and Ben weren't close. Ben was still trying to hit big flies, every time up, still striking out a lot, still willing to trade all those strikeouts for the occasional home run. But then, an awful lot of guys were willing to make that trade in the big leagues, Matt knew. It was why there were both record numbers of strikeouts and home runs at the exact same time.

But the team was winning. Matt didn't want that to change, even if he'd given up on Ben Roberson ever changing.

There were still times Matt would stutter at a game, often when he least expected it. It had happened in their most recent one, on the road, against the Roland Orioles, in the sixth inning of a game the Astros were winning 3–2. The last two runs that night had come as a result of a line-drive, two-run homer from Matt over the left field fence.

But the Orioles had a runner on first, the potential tying run, in the bottom of the sixth with Pat McQuade trying to close out another win for them. Matt called time and headed for the mound. José was sick tonight and so Kyle was playing shortstop, not his natural position.

Matt thought if there was a comebacker to Pat, the simplest was for him to take the throw at second, even though there was a left-handed hitter up and usually the shortstop covered second when there was a left-handed hitter.

And even though Matt wasn't going to say this to Pat, he thought his arm would give them the best chance at a double play, because he knew the hitter, the Orioles catcher, wasn't much of a runner.

It wasn't a big thing. But in a one-run game, Matt just wasn't taking any chances. He wanted everybody on the same page. Sarge always told them to be thinking one move ahead, instead of one behind.

But when Matt got to the mound, he locked up.

All he wanted to say was this:

"Ball back to you, I got the throw."

Just that.

Simple, right?

Not so much, not right now.

"B-b-b . . ."

That was all he had. He felt as if his lips had suddenly been glued together.

Now? he thought.

Now?

He could feel his face getting red. But he couldn't just walk away without saying anything. He tried to breathe through his nose, another exercise Ms. Francis had taught him.

Nothing.

Pat McQuade didn't say anything either, respecting Matt's wishes about guys not finishing his sentences. But this was one of those times when Matt wanted to tell Pat there were exceptions to every rule.

"B-b-b . . ."

He could see the ump coming out from behind home plate, wanting to break up the meeting, even if it hadn't been any kind of meeting at all. Matt looked over to Ben at first base, hoping Ben could see the helplessness in his eyes. But Ben just turned and walked back to the bag and stood next to the Orioles runner. Maybe he knew what was happening, maybe not. If he did, he wasn't doing anything about it.

"Hey, guys," the ump said now, "we about done here?"

Matt nodded.

Finally, *finally*, he said to Pat, "Throw to me on a ball back to you."

"Okay," Pat said. Then, "You okay?"

"Now I am," Matt said.

He ran back to second, breathing way too hard, as if he'd just run around *all* the bases. And then didn't have to worry about a ball being hit back to Pat, or to anybody else, because Pat struck out the next two Orioles batters to end the game.

When Matt got to the mound to congratulate him, he was able to speak properly, and smile.

"Thanks for pitching *me* out of a jam," Matt said.

THIRTY-THREE

Matt and Ms. Francis were in her office the afternoon after his brief melt at the end of the Astros–Orioles game.

"What were you feeling in that moment?" she said.

"Dumb as a rock," Matt said.

"Now, you know better than that," she said, and smiled at him. "The only thing that's ever dumb is thinking of yourself as dumb. This *isn't* dumb. This is you. This happens to you. We just need to be as smart as we can understanding it."

"Okay, I didn't feel dumb," he said. "I felt frustrated. And angry. It's like when I was walking over to talk to Pat I got tackled from behind." He felt himself biting on his lower lip. "And you know who tackled me? *Me.*"

Matt told her about Pat waiting for him to get the words out, thinking that's what he was supposed to do. He told her about looking over at Ben, and Ben turning away.

"You think he knew you were stuck?" she said.

"No clue," Matt said. "If he did, maybe he thought he was just following my rules, too."

"Did you ask him about it afterward?"

Matt shook his head.

"Well," she said, "let's look for some positives. As painful as the moment was, you managed to power through."

"Barely," Matt said. "Maybe I should carry a pen and paper in my back pocket, so I can write a note next time."

She was still smiling. She was the one who always seemed to power through.

"Come on," she said. "You know we don't talk nearly as much about melts, as you call them, as we used to."

"I guess."

"You *know.*"

He looked over at the wall to his right, at the poster Ms. Francis loved and so did Matt, of the Astros running on the field to celebrate after they had taken Game Seven from the Dodgers and won their first World Series. The last ball that night, he always told himself, had been hit to José Altuve, smallest guy on the field. The MVP of that World Series, he reminded himself constantly, was George Springer, who accepted the MVP trophy without stuttering one time.

"I don't want to be like this!" he said, the words coming out of him hot, and embarrassingly loud, followed quickly by, "I-I . . . I'm sorry."

Sometimes it was like that for him. A quick stop and start.

"You can yell your head off if it makes you feel better," Ms. Francis said. "It just won't change who you are. A great kid. A great baseball player. A great friend, when people give you half a chance. That's you. That's Matt."

She always had a glass of water for him. He drank some now.

"Getting back to last night," he said, "I think that maybe some of it had to do with being pressed for time. You go to the mound, you know you don't just get to stay there and chat for as long as you feel like it."

She grinned. "Maybe you should start the conversation on your *way* to the mound next time."

"Great," he said. "When I can talk, people will think I'm talking to myself."

"But talking!"

"Funny," Matt said.

"I have my moments," she said. Then she said, "If Ben had come over to the mound, what would you have said to him at that moment?"

"Help," Matt said in a quiet voice.

"Everybody needs some from time to time," she said.

"What, you're telling me I should still be trying to help out Ben?" Matt said. "He never asks."

"Not everybody does," she said.

THIRTY-FOUR

With one game left in the regular season, the Astros were 12–1. So much had happened across those thirteen games, on and off the field, not all of it good for Matt, not all of it good for Ben Roberson. Even their parents had become a big part of the story of the season, in a good way with Matt's mom, not so good with Ben's dad.

But Matt's mom had always said that parents were never supposed to be a big part of the story in Little League.

For as long as he could remember, her message about that had never changed:

"The games aren't about us. They're about you."

Even after Matt's latest session with Ms. Francis, he hadn't done anything to reach out to Ben. At their game the next night, the one that got them to 12–1, they had only talked about the game, and not very much about that. But Ben had hit a long home run in the sixth inning, in a game the Astros were already winning 7–2.

"That's the swing we're looking for," Ben's dad said when Ben was rounding first base, the ball already over the fence, him into his home run trot.

Matt knew what Mr. Roberson was saying, and knew that his mom knew, as well. This was the swing he'd taught his son, not the one Matt's mom had tried to teach him. What Matt really heard from Mr. Roberson was this:

Do it my way, not hers.

It didn't matter to Mr. Roberson that Ben had struck out all his other times up tonight against the Newbury Royals. Or that he'd left runners on base every time he did strike out. Or that when he finally did hit one out, it was a solo home run in what was already a blowout game. That didn't seem to matter to anybody in the Astros family after the game was over.

They just wanted to talk about how far Ben's ball had gone.

MIKE LUPICA

Matt was happy for him. He was starting to look at Ben the way Ben looked at his dad: He wanted baseball to make him happy. Hitting home runs was obviously a huge part of that. Maybe the only part.

As Ben crossed home plate, Matt decided he was going to ride his bike over to Ben's house and see, once and for all, if the two of them could figure things out, no matter which way Ben wanted to swing at baseballs.

Once and for all, he wanted to find out if they could be friends.

Matt knew that Ben lived on Lenox Avenue, on the other side of Healey Park from where Matt and his mom lived, much closer to downtown South Shore.

It was a longer bike ride than the one to Healey, but not crazy long. When Matt told his mom what his plan was, she said, "Are you sure you want to do this?"

"Wait a second," Matt said. "Aren't you the one who's always telling me that guys don't share their feelings and stuff?"

"That would be me," she said. "But I think that the real reason Ben has pulled back from you, and maybe everybody, is *because* of his dad. And if that's the case, and no matter how good your intentions are, I think you might be talking to the ocean here."

"I just want him to know I have his back off the field, too," Matt said.

"Even though you're not always sure that he has yours?"

Matt shrugged and put his hands out to the side, palms up.

"I don't know, Mom," he said. "Maybe we've just got as different ideas about what it means to be a friend as we do about hitting a baseball."

She was on her way to the newspaper for the next few hours. She had made Matt a sandwich and left it in the refrigerator, even though Matt said he was capable of making his own sandwich.

"You don't even want to make sure he's home before you head over there?" she said.

"Nah," he said. "He might tell me not to come."

"You might be making the trip for nothing," she said.

"Who's always telling me that you have to at least try to do the right thing?"

"You make me feel as if I'm debating myself here," she said.

Matt said, "You gotta know that I watch every move you make."

"Hope this move is a good one."

"Same," he said.

"Things have been kind of calm lately," she said. "I just don't want this to be a solution looking for a problem."

MIKE LUPICA

"Mom," Matt said, "I got this."

"You know what you want to say to him?"

"I kind of do," Matt said. "Now I just gotta make sure I'm able to say it."

Ben's dad answered the door.

"You looking for Ben?" he said.

Not "hello." Not "Hey, Matt." Just that.

"Yes, sir," Matt said.

"Ben didn't say anything about anybody coming over," Mr. Roberson said. "He knows I'm working at home today."

"I didn't tell him I was coming over," Matt said. "I was just out on my bike."

It wasn't a lie. He *was* out on his bike, even though he made it sound kind of random when it was the opposite of that. He was here because he wanted to be here. But he wanted to talk to Ben, not his dad.

"Well, Ben rode his bike into town to pick up some things for me at the pharmacy," Mr. Roberson said. "You just missed him."

Matt didn't know what Ben's dad did for a living, or what kind of work he was doing from home. But his mom did the same thing all the time. Maybe he was working more from home these days because Mrs. Roberson had moved out.

He was wearing a gray Yankees T-shirt and cargo shorts and

unlaced white sneakers. Standing right in front of Matt this way, he looked as big as his own house.

"You want to wait for him?" Mr. Roberson said finally.

"Do you know how long Ben might be?"

"Shouldn't be too long," he said. "You can wait inside if you want."

"Out here is fine," Matt said.

He didn't know whether he was afraid of Mr. Roberson, or just intimidated by him, or a little bit of both. He wished it had been Ben who'd answered the door, because he could feel himself running out of nerve with the things he wanted to say to Ben, things he'd been rehearsing in his head on the way over here.

He had nothing for his dad, who suddenly said, "I'm not so bad you know," as if he'd been reading Matt's mind.

Matt was still staring up at him, but didn't know how to respond. So he didn't say anything at all.

"I know what your mom must think of me," he said. "But the problem, at least the way I see it, is that we just have different philosophies about baseball. And I still think that if the situation in that one game had been reversed, and I was the one coaching, she would have been looking out for you the way I looked out for my kid."

Matt didn't plan to say what he said next. It just came out

of him. Sometimes he stopped, sometimes he couldn't stop himself.

"No, sir," he said.

"No sir . . . *what?*"

He took a deep breath. Now there was really no stopping.

"My mom has never called out one of my coaches," Matt said. "Ever."

"All due respect, son," Mr. Roberson said. "But she's not a coach just because Sarge stuck her down there at first base."

Just turn around and leave, Matt told himself. *This was a mistake, coming here. Just get on your bike and go.*

Matt didn't do that.

"All due respect to you, Mr. Roberson," he said. "But my mom is ten times the coach you think she is."

If his mom could stand up to him, so could he. Probably it was another thing he got from her.

Mr. Roberson surprised him then.

He smiled.

The only times he'd ever seen him smile was when Ben would go deep.

"You're as tough as my kid says you are," he said to Matt.

"Thanks," Matt said.

"That impresses me, you sticking up for your mom that way," Mr. Roberson said.

Matt wasn't trying to impress him. But he didn't say that.

"Tell you the truth," Mr. Roberson said, "I wish my boy was more like you. I know he looks strong enough to kick a hole in the outfield wall. But the boy's so soft sometimes. I call it soft, anyway. His mom says he's just sensitive."

He put air quotes around "sensitive."

"I don't see Ben that way," Matt said.

Now he was sticking up for Ben, to his own dad.

"You don't know him the way I do," Mr. Roberson said.

Then they both heard:

"No, you don't. Know me, I mean."

The street behind the Robersons' house was closest to town. Ben must have come home that way, and just walked his bike across their backyard. And there he was, holding a white plastic CVS bag, staring at his dad.

"Maybe that's our real problem, Dad," Ben said. "I'm sensitive and you're not nearly sensitive enough."

"I don't appreciate your tone," Mr. Roberson said.

"Well I guess that makes us even," Ben said. "I don't appreciate what you just said about me."

He took a few more steps, and handed the bag to his dad. "Here's your stuff," he said.

Then Ben turned to Matt.

"You want to get out of here?" he said.

"Sure," Matt said. "Where do you want to go?"

"Anywhere," Ben said.

He walked back to where he'd left his bike near their garage. He rode it down the driveway, stopping where Matt had left his. Then without another word between them, they started riding up Lenox Avenue.

They could hear Mr. Roberson yelling for Ben to come back.

But in that moment, he was talking to the ocean.

THIRTY-FIVE

Matt suggested they just go back to his house. Ben said that was fine with him.

"You like being there, right?" Ben said. "Your house?"

"Well, yeah."

"I don't like being in mine right now," Ben said.

"Isn't your dad going to be mad that you just rode away like that?" Matt said.

"He's mad about everything else," Ben said. "He might as well add that to his list."

Matt's mom wasn't home yet from the *Dispatch*. So he texted her and told her that he and Ben had just decided to head back. He could explain later why they had, and what had happened at Ben's house.

Matt got them both bottles of water out of the refrigerator. He asked if Ben wanted something to eat. Ben said he was fine. Matt asked if Ben wanted to go out in the backyard and throw a ball around. Ben said that sounded like a good idea to him, he needed to be outside and moving around. Matt went and got his glove, which always had a ball in the pocket, from his room and his mom's from the front hall.

Matt handed his mom's glove to Ben. He took the ball out of his own glove. The ball felt really good in his hand at that moment. Matt knew that baseball wasn't going to change what had happened and what had been said between Ben and his dad. Baseball wasn't going to make things a whole lot better.

But it sure wasn't going to make them worse.

As they were walking out to the yard, Ben said, "You think your mom is going to be here soon?"

Matt said he was pretty sure that she was.

"Good," Ben said. "I could kind of use a mom right now."

・・・

When Rachel Baker got home from the paper, Matt and Ben took turns telling her what had happened. Matt went first, relaying the conversation he'd had with Ben's dad before Ben came back from CVS. Ben picked it up there.

They were all sitting on the back patio, glasses of lemonade in front of them on the table.

"You have to understand something," Matt's mom said to Ben. "Sometimes people think it's in their best interest to act their strongest when they're feeling weakest." She smiled. "Men more often than women."

"But I know he thinks that about me," Ben said. "That I'm weak. I think the only time I'm strong enough for him is when I'm hitting home runs."

She said, "And when does he seem to think you're weakest?"

"When I talk about how much I miss my mom," Ben said.

As big as he was, the way he said that made him sound to Matt like a little boy. One who wanted his mom.

"Do you still talk to her?" Matt's mom said.

"Just about every day," Ben said. "But I try not to do it when my dad's around. If he hears me in my room talking to somebody, even if it's not her, he comes in after and asks if I was talking to her. That's what he calls her now. He doesn't ask me if I was talking to my mom. Just 'her.'"

Ben closed his eyes, let out some air. "And if he knows that I have talked to her, he always wants to know the same thing," he said. "What she said about him."

Matt was watching his mom, seeing what a good listener she was, how she was getting him to open up to her.

"You understand that adults can act out same as children do, right?" she said. "He's hurting right now, and he's angry."

"At her," Ben said.

"But she's not here," Matt's mom said. "And you are."

"But this isn't my fault!" Ben said.

"He knows that," she said.

"He doesn't act like he knows it," Ben said. "He just wants me to be as mad at her as he is."

"But you're not," she said.

"I just miss her," Ben said. "The only thing that makes me really angry is her being gone."

He stopped then. Suddenly his eyes were big and red. Matt didn't want him to cry, and knew how much Ben didn't want to cry in front of them.

Matt would have felt the same way.

"I don't think she's coming back," Ben said.

Matt's mom said, "You don't know that."

"What I know," Ben said, "is that sometimes she acts as angry at him as he is at her."

"With you caught in the middle."

Ben looked at her. Matt still thought he might start crying.

"When Matt's dad left," Ben said, "were you mad at him?"

She turned and looked at Matt now, and smiled at him, even though he knew this wasn't close to being one of her happy smiles.

"Sad," she said. "Sad for this guy, mostly. That he was going to grow up without a dad present in his life."

"Mom," Matt said, "you know I'm fine with that."

"Matt and I are both fine with it now," she said. "But I'm not going to lie to you, Ben. It wasn't easy, especially at first, trying to be two parents at once. Took me awhile to understand that I didn't have to be."

They sat there in silence then. Matt sipped some lemonade. So did Ben, who finally said, "I can't be what he wants me to be."

"But you can be there for him," she said.

"I don't even want to be *with* him right now," Ben said. "Nothing I do is right. Nothing I say is right."

"Maybe the best place is to remind him that you love him," Matt's mom said, "but that the one hurting the most right now is you."

"Mrs. Baker," Ben said, "do you really think that will help?"

"It can't hurt," she said.

She told him then that he was welcome to stay for dinner,

but that he'd have to clear it with his dad first. Ben said he would. But before he did, he wanted to ask her for a favor.

"Would you mind going over to the park and pitching to me a little bit?" he said. "Would that be okay?"

She turned to Matt. "Did he just ask me if it was okay for us all to play ball?"

"Pretty sure he did," Matt said.

"And did he act as if I would be the one doing *him* a favor?"

"Yup," Matt said.

Then she jumped up from the table and said this would give her a good chance to break in her new baseball shoes.

They all did some throwing when they got to the park. Ben asked Matt if he wanted to do some hitting, too. Matt said no, he was good, he was happy to shag balls in the outfield. Before he did, he and Ben dragged the pitching screen out in front of the mound.

"One question," Matt's mom asked Ben. "Are we gonna do this your way, or mine?"

"Yours," he said.

Then she took Matt's bat out of his hands, got into her own batting stance, and exaggerated the toe-tapping move she'd shown him before. Matt sat in the outfield grass and watched them.

She handed the bat back to him, got a few feet away, and acted as if she were throwing an imaginary ball. Ben showed her the short stride she wanted. Then she made him repeat it about a half-dozen times, throwing one imaginary pitch after another.

When she was satisfied, she went back to the mound, and began throwing real baseballs again. Ben missed the first few. But then he began connecting. The swing was better. Not a lot more compact. But shorter than it had been before.

He started to connect. There was a line drive to left, then another. He didn't step out of the box. Matt knew there were a couple of dozen balls in the ball bag, and Ben acted as if he wanted to swing at every one of them. Pretty soon Matt was chasing down balls from left field all the way to the right field line on the back field at Healey.

He was picking one up in right when Ben blasted one off the top of the wall in dead center. Even from out here, Matt could see the smile on Ben's face. And he thought: *If I were feeling it right now the way he is, I'd be happy too.*

Matt watched him and wondered when the last time was that Ben felt this happy, and relaxed, on a ball field.

Or anywhere.

Finally, knowing they had to be getting to the bottom of the bag, Ben hit one a mile to left-center, over Matt, over the wall, in the general direction of the ice cream truck parked in its usual spot near the field where they played their games.

And then Ben was the one dropping his bat the way the little boy Christopher had that day with his dad. Then it was Ben tearing around the bases, pumping his arms over his head as he did, laughing all the way.

Matt watched him go, and wished Ben's dad were here to see him.

Maybe he'd be happy himself for a change.

THIRTY-SIX

Ben stayed for dinner. They didn't talk about his dad any more, or his mom. They talked about baseball, about hitting and the Astros' last regular season game, and about the playoffs, in which the Astros had already clinched the top seed.

As they did, Matt thought about everything that had happened since he'd gotten on his bike and made the trip over to Ben's house. But even with everything that happened after that, he knew he would have signed up for what was happening right now at the dinner table:

He and Ben sitting around like this and talking the way friends did.

When it was time for Ben to leave, he said he would text Matt later and tell him how the big talk he planned to have with his dad had gone.

Only he didn't text, or call that night, or the next day. He didn't respond to the text Matt sent him.

Then he didn't show up for the Astros' practice, their last before their game against the North Shore Phillies. Sarge said Ben's dad had called and said that Ben was grounded.

"Did he say why?" Matt said, even though he was pretty sure he knew why.

"Just said that it was something between him and his son," Sarge said.

"Is he going to get to play against the Phillies?" Matt said.

"I didn't ask," Sarge said, "and he didn't say."

All Matt could think about was his mom having told Ben to make sure to tell his dad that he loved him, no matter what. Now Matt wondered if Ben had even done that. And if he had, it didn't seem to have helped him very much.

Matt's mom was late for practice, having had to stay longer at the paper than she'd anticipated. As soon as she got there, Matt told her about Ben being grounded.

"Because he left the way he did with you," she said.

"Nothing else makes sense," Matt said.

On the way home in the car, his mom asked if he'd told Sarge about the scene at Ben's house. He said he hadn't. It wasn't his place to talk about what Ben's dad had said about Ben not being strong enough. And, Matt told his mom, even if Sarge knew, it wasn't going to change anything anyway.

"I tried to go over there yesterday to help him," Matt said, "and got him into so much more trouble that now I *really* have to find a way to help him."

"Maybe the best way to help him right now is by doing one of the hardest things in the world for you," she said. "And for me, by the way."

"What?"

"Being patient," she said. "Because for now we've both done as much as we can."

"It wasn't enough," Matt said.

"It's just like sports," she said. "Sometimes your best isn't enough."

She said she was sure that Matt would hear from Ben, maybe as early as tonight. He did. Ben called while they were still in the car and said he wasn't allowed to play against the Phillies, and might not get to play at all for the rest of the season.

. . .

"This isn't fair!" Matt said when they were in the house.

"Sounds as if things haven't been too fair for Ben for a while," she said.

"This is all my fault," he said.

"No," she said, "it most certainly is not."

He wanted to go straight upstairs to his room. But his mom sat down on the bottom step of the stairs and said, "Step into my office."

He sat down next to her.

"Mom," he said, "before you say anything else, you have to know that if I hadn't gone over there, none of this would have happened."

Neither one of them had taken off their baseball shoes. She was still wearing her Astros cap—not the one she'd bought, but the one that Sarge had given her.

"You told me to leave well enough alone and I didn't listen," Matt said. "And now I might have cost Ben his season."

"No," she said, "the only one who can do that is his father."

"So we need to talk to him," Matt said, "and make things right."

"He's the boy's father," she said.

"He's still wrong," Matt said. "You could make him see that. You're good at stuff like that."

"I've probably said more to Ben than I should have already," she said. "And that probably hasn't helped him out much with his father, either."

"He has to let him play," Matt said.

"And I'm still hopeful he will," she said.

"When?"

"When he gets over himself," his mom said.

Matt went up to his room then, closed the door, opened his laptop, went to MLB Network, found a game between the Yankees and the Nationals. Gleyber Torres had become another young second baseman Matt loved to watch. But Matt couldn't focus on Torres, or on the game. His mind kept wandering to the same place: Ben's house.

Ben's dad was angry at his mom and now he was taking that out on Ben, and not letting him play ball. Great, Matt thought. It was grown-ups who acted like children sometimes, especially when the grown-ups were the ones who couldn't get their way.

What would Mr. Roberson do if the Astros won the league championship and made it to the state tournament? Would he make Ben miss that, too?

But Matt didn't want Ben to miss even one game.

He had to do something. He had to do something, or his mom did, or both of them. Ben's dad was wrong. They *did* have to do something to make things right. He closed his laptop, leaned back, rested his head against the pillows he'd propped up behind him, underneath his José Altuve poster.

Altuve was his baseball hero, an undersize guy with all that power.

Right now, Matt didn't feel as if he had any.

He tried telling himself that they were just baseball games. That it was just baseball. But in his heart, he knew it was about a lot more than that.

THIRTY-SEVEN

The Astros won their game against the Phillies without Ben. He had texted Matt a couple of hours before the game started to tell him that he definitely wouldn't be there, that his dad hadn't changed his mind.

Ben: Still baseball grounded.
Matt: U ok?
Ben: Just bummed.

Matt: Can u come over?

Ben: No

Matt: U off team for good?

Ben: TBD

Matt: ???

Ben: To be determined.

Matt: Call whenever.

Ben: Dad doesn't want me talking to you right now.

Matt: U gotta play playoffs.

Ben: Right now gotta bounce.

The Cubs, the only team to have beaten the Astros, ended up in fourth place, so the Astros would play them in one semifinal game. The other semi would be between the Glenallen Giants, Joey the big-mouth catcher's team, and the Mariners.

The Astros had beaten the Cubs in the teams' second meeting of the season, but Andrew Welles, their star, hadn't pitched that game. They would be facing him on Tuesday night.

"That guy Andrew is a beast," José said to Matt on practice Monday night.

"So are we," Matt said. "What's the Spanish word for beast?"

"*Bestia.*"

"Perfect way to describe us," Matt said. "The word even has 'best' in it."

"We need to be the best *bestia* in the league for two more games," José said.

His face turned serious, and so did his tone.

"Can we do that without Ben being dangerous in the middle of our order?" he said.

"I keep telling myself there's no way his dad won't let him play the playoffs," Matt said.

"It's like you said," José told Matt. "His dad is hurting and now Ben is the one *getting* hurt."

By now Matt had filled José in on what was going on at Ben's house. He knew José well enough to know he wouldn't tell anybody else, after Matt made him promise not to. And Matt just wanted to talk about Ben's situation with somebody other than his mom. It's what friends did. They tried to help each other figure things out, even though Matt wasn't doing much good in that area for Big Ben.

It was their normal practice that night, just without the occasional long ball from Ben. Matt's mom worked with the infielders, as always, and was as enthusiastic with them as if this was the first day of practice for All-Stars after the team had been set. The only difference between tonight and that night was that Chris Conte was at first base, not Ben Roberson.

After Sarge finished pitching batting practice tonight, the guys started to pack up. But then Sarge told them there was one more hitter.

"Sarge," Matt said, "we all hit."

Sarge grinned.

"Yeah," he said. "But she hasn't hit yet."

He was pointing at Matt's mom.

"We saw what you had when you pitched against one of my guys," Sarge said. "You want to show what you got against me?"

Matt's mom didn't hesitate. She walked calmly over to the bench, grabbed Matt's batting helmet and his bat, and started walking toward the plate, taking quick cuts with Matt's bat as she did.

When she got into the batter's box she said, "Not afraid to get shown up by a girl?"

"I'm man enough to risk it," Sarge said.

She pointed the bat at him, and tried to look menacing, which Matt knew was pretty much impossible for his mom.

"Don't you go easy on me," she said.

"Didn't even cross my mind," Sarge said.

Matt watched his mom step out and take a few more practice swings, as Stone Russell, who'd quickly put his chest protector and mask back on, got behind the plate. Then she took her stance. Matt smiled. It looked exactly like his stance.

Sarge threw a pitch away. She let it go. The ball hadn't missed being a strike by much. Just enough.

"You trying to get me to chase," she called out to Sarge as Stone threw the ball back to him.

"Just establishing what you think is a strike," he said.

"When it's a strike," she said, "I'll let you know."

She did on the very next pitch. The ball was at her knees. Matt thought it would have definitely caught the outside corner, which is where Stone had set up. The ball never got to his mitt. Matt's mom went with the pitch, and got herself a clear, solid knock to right field.

Matt's mom couldn't help herself. She started running to first base as soon as she dropped the bat.

Halfway down the line, she stopped.

"Old habits," she said.

"Oldies but goodies," Sarge said.

"Like us," Matt's mom said.

When everyone else was gone, Matt and his mom and Sarge sat on the Astros bench and talked about Ben.

"I love that kid," Sarge said, "which is just one more reason why I hate to see what he's going through."

"I still can't believe he won't let him come back and play," Matt's mom said.

"He's pretty stubborn," Sarge said.

He was rolling a baseball around in his hands. Once practice started, Sarge always seemed to have a ball in his hand.

"Not as stubborn as I am," Matt's mom said.

"Now that you told me what happened," Sarge said, "I can't believe he's going to ruin the boy's summer over that. And I can't just sit by and *let* him ruin the boy's summer over that."

He stood up.

"I'm gonna head over and have a talk with him, whether he wants to or not," Sarge said.

Matt's mom stood too. She reached over, took the ball out of Sarge's hand, rubbed it up, handed it back to him.

"I'll go," she said.

"Not your job," Sarge said.

"Maybe it is," she said. "Maybe it's time Bob and I had a man-to-man talk."

She smiled.

"Or mom-to-man," Matt said.

"Either way," she said.

THIRTY-EIGHT

They didn't even stop home to change out of their baseball gear. They went straight to the Robersons' house. Matt's mom said this couldn't wait.

"You told me to wait," Matt said.

"I was wrong," she said, then smiled and shrugged. "Happens from time to time. I should have gone over there as soon as Ben missed his first practice."

"I'm glad you're letting me come, too," Matt said.

"We're a team, remember?"

Matt said, "Now we have to get Ben back on it."

They made the turn on Lenox Avenue, and pulled up in front of the house.

"You know," she said, "this all kind of started when I benched Ben that night. All I'm trying to do now is un-bench him."

They saw Mr. Roberson's car in the driveway. So he was home. As they walked up the front walk, Matt felt a little bit like he was walking up to home plate.

His mom rang the bell. Mr. Roberson must have either heard them pull up, or seen them walking toward the door, because he opened it right away.

It was open just enough that Matt could see Ben standing halfway down the stairs behind his dad.

"I have to tell you," Mr. Roberson said, "that I don't appreciate you coming over here without calling first. Apparently it's a thing in your family."

"We need to talk, Bob," Matt's mom said.

"I have nothing to say to you."

"Dad," Ben said.

Mr. Roberson didn't even turn around.

"Go back to your room, Ben," he said. "This doesn't involve you."

"Yes," Matt's mom said, "it does."

They all stood there, like they were frozen in place. Ben was still halfway down the stairs. His dad was in the doorway, hand on the knob. Matt and his mom were on the front porch.

No one said anything until Matt's mom spoke again.

"You're acting like an idiot, Bob," she said. "Now please let us come inside so we can talk about this."

To Matt's amazement, that is exactly what Mr. Roberson did.

THIRTY-NINE

Mr. Roberson didn't offer them anything to drink. Matt and his mom, and Ben, just followed him into the living room. From a television in another room, Matt could hear the sound of a baseball game.

Ben and his dad sat on the couch. Matt and his mom sat in chairs across from them, with an old wood coffee table in between them. And maybe about a thousand miles.

"I have to say again," Ben's dad said, "I still don't appreciate you just showing up this way. How would you feel if I came to your house unannounced?"

"If it was important, and it was about my son," she said, "I'd thank you."

"I'm raising my son," he said. "You raise yours. I believe that's the way it still works."

"Oh, please!" Rachel Baker said. "I wish it were that easy. Maybe you haven't heard, but these days it takes a village."

"What does that even mean?" Ben's dad said.

"It *means*," she said, "that we're all in this together where our children are concerned."

She smiled at him, the best one she had.

"Why exactly did you ground Ben?" she said. "I'm curious."

"That really is between Ben and me."

"Oh come on, Dad!" Ben said. "You grounded me because I rode off on my bike with Matt that day."

"It was just a part of it," Mr. Roberson said.

"B-b-b . . ."

"But." Matt wanted to start with that.

Come on, loser!

He knew Ms. Francis hated it when he called himself a loser. But he felt like one now.

Don't stop there.

"B-but that makes me a part of it," Matt said.

"Matt's right," his mom said. "We're all a part of this. And why all of us need to find a way to get past this."

"I told my son to stay," Ben's dad said. "He chose to leave. I'm his father. I can't have him disobeying me that way." He leaned forward and looked at Matt's mom then and said, "You can at least understand that, right?"

"What I understand, Bob," she said, still smiling at him, "is that you need to lighten up."

"I'm his father!"

Matt's mom leaned forward now, and her voice was as soft as his had been loud.

"Then start acting like one," she said.

Mr. Roberson started to say something, but then seemed to think better of it. He took a deep breath instead, and slowly let it out.

Like one of my exercises, Matt thought.

It was Ben who spoke next.

"Dad," he said, "please listen to her."

"Whose side are you on?" his dad said.

"We're all on Ben's side," Matt's mom said.

"Oh, I get it," Mr. Roberson said. "You're going to teach me about parenting the way you think you can teach my son how to hit a baseball."

"No," she said. "I know how hard it is to be a parent. And I know how hard it is to be a single parent, because I learned that myself. The hard way. It's what you're experiencing right now. But I've learned something along the way, and it's something I tell my own son all the time."

"What's that?" Mr. Roberson said.

"That there's no shame in asking for help," she said.

"But I didn't ask for your help," he said.

"It doesn't mean I can't offer it," she said.

Matt saw Mr. Roberson's face getting red. He could see how tightly he was gripping his knees with his big hands.

"You don't know what it's like," he said.

"But that's the thing," she said. "I do."

Mr. Roberson turned and nodded at Ben. "If I don't let him know that actions have consequences," he said, "then I'm not doing my job."

"But what about your actions, Dad?" Ben said.

"I-I-I . . ."

Suddenly it was Mr. Roberson who was stammering. He either didn't know what words to say—or couldn't say them.

Know the feeling, Matt thought.

"*I* can help," Matt's mom said. "We all can."

"It's not the way I was raised," Ben's dad said. "To ask for help."

"I know," Matt's mom said.

She stood. So did Matt.

"Please think about what was said here tonight," she said. "And think about what's best for your boy."

Before Mr. Roberson could answer, she said, "We'll show ourselves out."

Matt looked at Ben, who looked as if he wanted to leave with them, the way he'd left with Matt a few days ago.

At the doorway to the living room, Matt's mom turned around and said something Matt had heard her say plenty of times before.

"The games aren't about us, Bob," she said. "Let the boy play."

Then they left.

FORTY

The game with the Cubs was scheduled for six-thirty at Healy Park.

Waiting for a night game was always hard, especially when it was the biggest game of the year. It was just much worse today, because there had been what his mom called "radio silence" from Ben since last night.

His mom was working from home today. She was at her desk, in the small den off the kitchen she'd converted into an office. José was on his way over, and he and Matt were going into town to have lunch, just as a way of killing time before their game against the Cubs.

"I'll tell you again what I've been telling you since we got home last night," she said. "As often as the world disappoints me, I still expect that people will choose to do the right thing."

"But you said yourself that Ben's dad has put himself in a bad place," Matt said.

"Correct," she said. "But if he's being honest with himself, he knows that whatever crime he thinks Ben committed by showing him up, this punishment doesn't fit that crime. But all parents put themselves into that bad place from time to time, when they overreact."

Matt grinned.

"When I was little," he said, "it would start with a time-out and end up with me losing my television privileges."

She laughed. "And all other privileges!" she said. "You're right. I think that's what's happening here. What should have been a simple time-out turned into this. The problem is, we're now about to run out of time."

They heard the doorbell.

"Go have lunch," she said.

Matt and José rode their bikes into town, had sandwiches at the Candy Kitchen, and then walked around, trying to kill more of the time running out for Ben Roberson.

There was a moment, at the corner of Elm and Main, when Matt thought he saw Ben coming, but it wasn't him.

Around four o'clock, José rode his bike home. Matt did the same. They agreed to meet at Healey no later than five, because Matt knew he wouldn't be able to stay at home any longer than that, not just waiting for the game, but worrying about Ben.

There was no longer any doubt about the friendship he and Ben had formed. It was the strangest part of this, Matt thought: He'd worked so hard to gain a friend, and now he'd lost a teammate.

"He'll either be here or he won't," Matt's mom said when they got to the field. "We did everything we could."

Before too long, Sarge and the rest of his teammates were there. By five-thirty, the Cubs players were over on their side of the field. Matt told himself it was time to start focusing on their opponents, and not Ben, even though he couldn't stop thinking about what it would be like if someone had taken baseball away from him.

The Cubs got the field first, for fielding drills and then batting practice. Then it was the Astros' turn. When their fielding drills were over and it was time for their BP, Matt went over and asked his mom what time it was.

"Six-oh-five," she said, looking at her phone.

Matt shook his head. "He'd be here by now if we were coming," he said to her.

"Maybe so," she said, putting a hand on his shoulder.

"This stinks!" he said.

"So it does," she said. "But it doesn't change the fact that there's still a game to play."

"We need to win it for Ben," Matt said. "If we do, maybe his dad will change his mind before the championship game."

She squeezed his shoulder now.

"Have I mentioned lately that you're a good boy?" she said.

"You're prejudiced," he said.

"Even so," she said.

When they finished BP, Sarge gathered them together at their bench. He told them he had a few things to say, and promised that it would only be a few for once.

The Astros were all facing Sarge, and the field. He was kneeling in front of them, a baseball in his hand.

"Actually, I only have one big thing to say," Sarge said.

"Wait. Me first."

Even before Matt whipped his head around, he knew the voice belonged to Ben's dad.

"I just want to say I'm sorry we're late," Mr. Roberson said.

Ben was next to him, in his cap and Astros T-shirt. In his

spikes. Both he and his dad were out of breath.

"I thought the game was at seven o'clock," Mr. Roberson said.

Then he turned to Matt's mom, and almost seemed to be smiling.

"I'm an idiot," he said.

FORTY-ONE

Sarge told Ben there wasn't time for him to take batting practice. Ben grinned and said, "I had a pretty good session with Matt's mom the other day."

"So you're good to go?" Sarge said.

"*So* good," Ben said.

Then Sarge sat down at the end of the bench and ripped out the page in his scorebook with his batting order and wrote out a new one. Matt and Ben jogged down the right field line so

Ben could get some quick throwing in. Matt even threw him a few ground balls.

As they walked back to the bench, Matt said, "What happened?"

"We finally talked to each other," Ben said. "And listened."

"My mom says that works wonders," Matt said.

"Did this time with my dad," Ben said. "I'm here, right?"

Sarge was waving them back over to the bench, where the rest of the Astros and Matt's mom were waiting.

"As I was saying," Sarge said, "before Ben interrupted me."

As nervous and excited as they all were, it got a laugh out of them.

"I think we all just got reminded how important it is, to all of us, to be a part of a team," Sarge said. "You know we all got here together. Now we're more together than we've ever been."

He'd been kneeling. He stood up now.

"I know I'm ready for this," he said. "What about you guys? You ready?"

"*Yes!*" they shouted at him, with one loud voice.

Unfortunately, the opposing pitcher, Andrew Welles, was ready, too.

Very.

• • •

Andrew was everything they all remembered from the first game of the season, and more.

"I swear that guy has gotten bigger," José said after Andrew had retired him and Denzel and Matt in order in the bottom of the first.

"And better, maybe," Matt said.

Mike Clark was the Astros starter and shut down the Cubs over the first four innings, managing to pitch his way out of a bases loaded, nobody out jam in the second, finally striking out the Cubs shortstop.

But Andrew was dominating the Astros at the same time, pounding away at the strike zone, hardly ever wasting a pitch, even when he was ahead in the count. Through the bottom of the fourth, Matt had his team's only hit, having managed to carve a ground ball between the shortstop and second baseman his second time up. Ben had hit the ball hard twice using the simpler swing Matt's mom had taught him, but had nothing to show for it except two line drive outs, both to the center fielder.

It was still 0–0 going into the fifth.

Up until then, the only thing Matt had heard from Mr. Roberson, back in his usual spot, sitting in his lawn chair, was this, after both of Ben's outs:

"Good swing. One of them will fall in."

The Cubs scored first, in the top of the fifth. Mike, who

hadn't made many mistakes after the second inning, made one to Andrew with two outs and Jake McAuliffe, the Cubs catcher, on first. Mike left one up and over the plate and Andrew knew what to do with it, hitting a screamer between Denzel and Teddy to left-center. He ended up with a triple, and Jake scored easily. Mike struck out the next guy to leave Andrew at third. But it was 1–0.

The way Andrew was pitching, that "1" on the scoreboard looked like a "10" to Matt right now.

When they got back to the bench, ready to hit in the bottom of the inning, Matt's mom said, "May I make a comment?"

"Have at it," Matt said.

She looked around at Matt and his teammates, and just loud enough for them to hear she said, "We need to get that big guy throwing for them out of his comfort zone, or he's going to pitch those guys right into the championship game."

"How do we do that?" José said.

Matt's mom leaned down close to Stone, who was taking off his chest protector, his mask next to him on the bench.

"Stone," she said, "he falls pretty hard toward first base on his follow-through. How about you try laying down a bunt toward third?"

"Not a very good bunter, Mrs. B," he said.

"Be one now," she said. "It'll work. Their third baseman will be back, and guarding the line against a double. Trust me."

"Trust her," Matt said to Stone. "It's always worked for me."

Stone didn't wait. And the guy who said he wasn't much of a bunter laid down a beauty, dropping the bat at the very last second, deadening the ball just right, putting enough backspin on the ball that it died halfway up the line. By the time the third baseman picked the ball up with his bare hand, there was no point in making a throw. The second hit of the game for the Astros had traveled about thirty feet, tops.

Didn't matter.

Potential tying run at first, nobody out.

Matt looked down at his mom in the first-base coach's box. She was smiling across the field at Sarge. Usually he was the one giving the signs. Now she was giving them to him. And to Kyle Sargent.

Telling Kyle to lay one down as well.

Sarge nodded.

Matt liked it: Tie the game now if they could, worry about the go-ahead run later. First things first, now that Stone was at first.

Kyle, who *was* a good bunter, wasn't trying to surprise anybody. This was a sacrifice bunt all the way. He squared up, and then he was the one deadening the ball just right, in the direction of first. The first baseman, charging, fielded it. He had no chance to get Stone at second, so he just turned and threw to his second baseman, who was covering first behind him.

Now the tying run was at second.

But then Andrew Welles struck out Chris Conte with three pitches. Two outs. Teddy Sample at the plate. If the Astros got to the championship game, Teddy would be starting it. But they had to get there. And to get there, they needed runs, starting with the one standing at second in the person of Stone Russell.

Matt was sitting next to Pat McQuade, who was going in to pitch the sixth even if the Astros were still behind.

"This has to be Andrew's last inning," Pat said.

Matt said, "If we're ever going to get to this guy, we have to do it right here."

"Our ace against theirs," Pat said.

"Except ours is batting instead of pitching," Matt said.

Teddy didn't wait. He hit the first fastball he saw from Andrew Welles over second base and into center field. Stone, a catcher who could really run, easily beat the throw home.

Mike Clark struck out. But the game was 1–1 going into the top of the sixth. Pat needed to get them three outs, and then they'd try to get the run that got them to Saturday. Matt laid it out for Pat before he walked to the mound.

"Let me get this straight," Pat said. "I pitch a scoreless inning and then we get the winning run in the bottom of the last."

"Yup," Matt said.

"Promise?" Pat said.

Matt grinned up at him. Pat was a lot bigger than he was.

"You know what they say in that other sport," Matt said. "Ball don't lie."

He and Pat touched gloves.

"And neither do I," Matt said.

Pat did his job in the top of the sixth. The guy leading off for the Cubs, their right fielder, hit a slow roller in front of Matt, who had to make a barehanded throw to Ben and got the guy by a stride. Pat got two strikeouts after that. He'd only have to face Andrew Welles again if the game went to extra innings. But maybe it wouldn't if they could get a run off the Cubs closer, Robbie Gallo.

José was leading off the bottom of the sixth, then Denzel, and Matt. If one of them got on, Ben would get a chance. They had scored so many runs all season, in all kinds of ways. Now they just needed one more to keep playing.

José finally walked after a terrific at bat, fouling off three pitches after Robbie got the count to 3-2. Denzel bunted José to second. Jake, their catcher, was the one who fielded the ball, and thought about trying for José at second, then decided to make the safe play at first.

So now the potential winning run was on second for Matt, with one out.

Somehow, after all the things that had happened this season, on the field and off, he was exactly where he wanted to be and maybe where he was supposed to be.

He took the deep breaths Ms. Francis had taught him to take when he couldn't talk, in a moment where he didn't need to say anything.

All he had to do was hit.

"Don't wait for me," Ben said from the on-deck circle.

Robbie threw two pitches away, not close to being strikes. Maybe Robbie was going to walk Matt and take his chances with Ben, whom he'd gotten to weakly pop out to end the first game the two teams had played.

Or maybe Robbie was just trying to set up Matt away, and then come hard inside on him.

He did. Matt was ready, and jumped on the pitch, lining one over the leap of their shortstop and into left field. Matt was sure he'd won the game as he took off for first, watching their left fielder charge the ball as José rounded third.

Even if the guy fielded it cleanly, he wasn't going to get José.

Only José, who usually was a great baserunner, took too wide a turn at third.

Then he stumbled as he tried to get himself back closer to the baseline.

Stumbled and went down.

Matt watched from first as the left fielder threw behind José, as he barely crawled back to the bag right before Andrew Welles put the tag on him.

Matt could see how furious José was with himself, slapping the sides of his batting helmet with his hands. It wasn't going to change anything. The game was still 1–1.

For Ben.

"Good swing," Matt heard from behind him. Two voices, almost at the same moment. His mom's voice. And Ben's dad.

Matt thought: Maybe Ben is where he's supposed to be, too. Maybe this is the way things were supposed to work out for him, in a game he didn't even know he was going to get to play.

Ben took his stance, wider than it had been at the start of the All-Stars season. Matt's mom had told him that if his feet were just a little wider apart, he wouldn't over-stride as much.

Matt wanted his friend to get a hit almost as much as he'd wanted to get one himself.

Or more.

Ben took a ball. Then a strike.

Robbie tried to go up and away. Not far enough away. Ben waited on the pitch, not over-anxious at all, brought his left leg forward just a little, and absolutely smoked a ball over the first baseman's head and down the line and into the corner. José could have walked home with the run that put the Astros into the championship game.

Matt was at second when José crossed the plate, but then reversed himself, and started running back toward first, because that's where Ben was, already being mobbed by the rest of their teammates, all of them yelling their heads off.

Matt, though, was only talking to himself.

"Good swing," he said.

FORTY-TWO

Matt had a session with Ms. Francis the day before the championship game, which would be against the Giants and his pal Joey.

Matt told her everything that had happened since his last visit to her office.

"Sounds to me," she said, "as if you spoke up for Ben and then Ben spoke up for himself. You both found your voices."

"I know we've talked about this before," Matt said. "But at the start of the season I thought he had everything going for him, and then he was the one who went through more than I ever did."

"Then it was as if you both got the game-winning hit," she said. "Maybe it was good that José slipped."

"José doesn't exactly see it that way," Matt said.

"Also sounds to me," she said, "as if the stuttering has been more infrequent lately."

"It's still in me," Matt said. "I know it's always going to be. Maybe I've been too busy to think about it as much."

"Not thinking about it isn't such a terrible thing," she said. "But it doesn't mean we're going to stop working."

Matt grinned.

"I was afraid of that," he said.

"Before we go through our exercises," she said, "do me a favor. Tell me, in your own words, why you think this season has been so important to you."

"Being part of a team is always important to me," he said. "Every team I've ever been on."

"But this has to have been a particularly rewarding season," she said. "Tell me about that."

"If *you'd* told me about that, I could have written something down before I came," Matt said.

She smiled at him.

"Just speak from the heart," she said. "You hardly ever get tripped up doing that."

So he did.

FORTY-THREE

Championship Saturday.

The game was scheduled to start at eleven o'clock. The whole team was at Healey Park by nine-thirty, stretching in the outfield, then running from one line to the other, then doing some soft-tossing.

Matt was playing catch with Ben when he saw Mr. Roberson sitting down next to Matt's mom and Sarge on the Astros' bench. Mr. Roberson seemed to be doing most of the talking.

Matt walked over to Ben, and pointed.

"What do you suppose they're talking about?" he said.

"I know what my dad is saying," Ben said.

"What?"

"He's apologizing for the way he acted," Ben said.

He grinned.

"It was time for him to be the bigger person, finally," Ben said.

Sometimes it seemed to take forever to get from warm-ups to the first pitch. Not today. In a blink, Sarge was giving them his pregame talk.

"I just want you to go out and play a game we'll all always remember," Sarge said. "That sound all right to you guys?" He smiled, then held up a finger and said, "You guys and Matt's mom, I meant to say."

"Sarge," she said. "I was one of the guys the first time you let me on the field."

Then she turned to the Astros and said, "Let's get this party started," right before they all sprinted out onto the field to play the big game.

The only chuckleheaded moment from Joey came on Matt's first at bat. The Giants had gone out in order in the top of the first. José and Denzel had both grounded out ahead of Matt.

As Matt stepped into the batter's box, Joey said, "H-h-ow you d-d-oing, little dude?"

Matt didn't step out. Or look behind him.

He just laughed.

Loudly.

The home plate ump said, "What's so funny?"

Matt just gave a little nod at Joey and said, "Him."

Then he took his stance and doubled over the left fielder's head. Ben singled him home. It was 1–0. Matt didn't even look at Joey as he crossed home plate, even though he thought about it. Too much baseball still to be played. And that double had been enough of a response for now.

After Stone struck out to end the Astros' half of the first, Matt's mom said, "What was so funny up there?"

"The catcher made fun of my stuttering," Matt said.

"Were you?" she said. "Stuttering, I mean."

"Nah."

"But you laughed it off?"

"Mom," he said, "I've got other stuff to worry about."

The game stayed 1–0 into the fifth. Teddy was throwing better than he had all season and, even better than that, his pitch count was really low. There was no question that Sarge would send him out for the top of the fifth, telling Pat there was no need for him to even start warming up yet. Sarge was going to ask Teddy to get them three more outs, and then give the ball to Pat and ask him to close out the league season.

Teddy got the first two outs, then he walked their center fielder. It didn't seem to matter when the next guy hit what looked to be an easy grounder to José. Matt ran over to cover for what looked as if it would be a routine force, but the ball took a terrible hop, going high off José's chest. By the time he had his hand on the ball, everybody was safe.

Then Teddy gave up the hardest hit, by far, he'd given up in the game—a shot from their shortstop over Denzel's head in center. Matt fired a relay throw to the plate, trying to cut down the second run. Too late.

Just like that, it was Giants 2, Astros 1.

Teddy struck out the next batter. But damage done. Everything had changed with one swing of the bat, because that was baseball. Chris Conte, Mike Clark, Teddy—the bottom of their order—went out one-two-three in the bottom of the fifth. The game stayed 2–1. Pat struck out the side in the top of the sixth. What did that TV commercial say? Life comes at you fast. Everything seemed to be happening much too fast at Healey Park now.

Last ups for the Astros, top of the order, maybe for the last time this season if they couldn't at least tie things up: José, Denzel, Matt.

Matt, who was sitting at the end of the bench, turned around and saw Ms. Francis in the bottom row of the bleachers, smiling at him, as if she'd been waiting for him to see her there. Then she slowly brought her hands up, as if taking a big, deep breath, as if they were in her office.

Matt nodded and did the same, even though they were in *his* office now.

Then he turned back to the field and saw José, who promised Matt he was going to get a hit his next time up, still angry at himself even though the bad hop hadn't been his fault, drill a clean single to center.

Denzel hit a slow roller to first. Their first baseman made a neat play, closing on the ball quickly enough that he could get a tag on Denzel before Denzel was by him. But it was as good as a sacrifice bunt, because José made it to second.

So the tying run was standing right there. Matt walked around the ump and around Joey. He checked Sarge right before he stepped into the box. Then he looked down at his mom in the first-base coaching box.

She just smiled at him, and gave two quick pats to her heart.

Joey wasn't saying anything now. Matt probably wouldn't have heard him even if he had. He was that locked in. His mom had always told him to just focus on the moment, that everything else was just noise.

But Matt couldn't hear anything right now, except maybe the beating of his own heart.

The first pitch was high and tight and backed Matt off the plate. Maybe Joey had called for their closer to come inside on Matt that way, get his feet moving. Fine if he had. That was baseball, too. The next pitch was a called strike. Matt didn't think it had caught the corner. The ump said it had.

Matt swung over the next pitch.

Now it was 1-2.

"Only takes one," he heard Ben say from the on-deck circle.

That pitch came next. It was up and over the plate. Might have been a strike to someone as big as Big Ben. Not for Matt. He jumped on it anyway, caught it on the sweet spot, the ball high and deep toward right field.

Matt had gotten all of it. He was pretty sure it was over the right fielder's head even as the kid turned and chased. He was tracking the ball and so was Matt and so was everybody. It was going to be an extra-base hit at least. Matt was sure the game was about to be tied.

He kept following the ball with his eyes and was just about to first base when he saw the right fielder stop suddenly, his knees buckling, as the ball disappeared over the wall.

First walk-off home run of Matt Baker's life.

Astros 3, Giants 2.

He seemed to float the rest of the way around the bases. His teammates were waiting for him at the plate, jumping up and down, ready to mob him.

Halfway between third and home, Matt tossed his batting helmet away.

Just like the big guys did.

FORTY-FOUR

When the celebration on the field was finally over and they were all waiting for the presentation of the championship trophy, Ben said to Matt, "Someday you have to teach me how to hit a big fly like that."

They both laughed.

Matt's mom had been cool, just because he would have expected nothing less from her, when the game ended. She just stole a quick moment, gave him a hug, and told him how happy she was for him.

"I'd tell you that you made me proud," she said, "but you know that's not my style. You made yourself proud."

Sarge came over, shaking his head.

"All the way to the last pitch of the season," he said, "they just didn't get how hard you can hit a baseball."

Matt shrugged. "Looks can be deceiving, I guess," he said.

"Yeah," Sarge said. "They sure can."

He hugged Matt too.

When it was time for the ceremony, Sarge brought the Astros out and lined them up behind the pitcher's mound. There was a table set up in front of them, with the trophy on it. The spectators, all the parents and other relatives and friends, were standing in the home plate area, facing the Astros.

The president of the league spoke into the standing microphone that had been set up, congratulating both teams, talking about what a wonderful game of baseball they'd all just witnessed.

Then he called for Sarge to make a few comments, which he did, before the president handed him the trophy and Sarge hoisted it in the air, and they all heard one more big cheer on this day.

After Sarge placed the trophy back on the table, he stepped

up to the microphone, and said, "This trophy belongs to these players behind me. These games, and these seasons—and these memories—are about them."

He paused.

"In that spirit," he continued, "I would like to ask the boy who just won the game to step forward and make a few comments."

He turned.

"Matt," he said, "come on out here."

There was another cheer, this time from the Astros.

Just not from Matt.

He looked at Sarge and shook his head, not moving. He looked over at his mom then, and Ms. Francis, who happened to be standing next to her near home plate.

He saw Ms. Francis mouth these words:

You . . . can . . . do . . . this.

Maybe he could. He didn't want to.

Didn't want to speak in front of the team, not today.

José leaned over. "You got this," he said into Matt's ear, and gave him a gentle push toward the microphone.

Somehow Matt got his feet to start moving, as he saw Sarge lowering the microphone for him.

You've already got the words, Matt told himself.

You practiced yesterday in front of Ms. Francis.

Now Ms. Francis was standing right there in front of him, as if she was on the other side of the desk in her office.

Just say a little of what you said to her into the microphone.

All he had to do was tell everybody how proud he was to be a part of this team. How proud he was of the way they came back today.

How excited they all were to be going to the state tournament.

I'm proud to be an Astro.

Just start with that.

His mouth felt as dry as the dirt on the mound in front of him. He couldn't seem to take any air in. All the triggers, which is what Ms. Francis called them, were suddenly locked in, as he locked up.

Everybody looked at him, and waited.

"I-I-I . . ."

His mouth was wide open. But that was all that came out. He closed his eyes, feeling his face begin to redden, feeling helpless. He thought about how George Springer had managed to find all the words, perfectly, when he'd accepted the World Series MVP trophy, in front of the whole country that time.

Matt tried again.

Nothing.

Crickets.

It was then that he felt a hand on his shoulder.

Ben's.

Ben had come out to stand next to him.

He smiled at Matt and said, "Don't wait for me."

He took his hand away then, and stepped back, as Matt finally began to talk.